"Trust Me?"

Vanessa asked. "Just this once have faith in me that I'll do what's right for both of us?"

"Blind trust," Seth muttered, uncertain he was capable of trusting anyone.

Hearing the wariness in his voice, she replied. "Yes. Trust. It's the cornerstone of love."

Seth felt a flash of childhood panic. He'd been forced to rely only upon himself. She was asking for more than his love. She wanted him to relinquish the control it had taken for him to make his own fate. Figuratively, he'd be handing his heart over to her to do with as she chose. His survival instincts rose in his mind, issuing a loud warning: *Trust her and you'll have nothing left if she betrays you!*

A wry smile raised  so much, he wouldr her. . . .

Dear Reader:

It takes two to tango, and we've declared 1989 the "Year of the Man" at Silhouette Desire. We're honoring that perfect partner, the magnificent male, the one without whom there would be no romance. From January to December, 1989 will be a twelve-month extravaganza, spotlighting one book each month as a tribute to the Silhouette Desire hero—our *Man-of-the-Month*!

You'll find these men created by your favorite authors utterly irresistible. March, traditionally the month that "comes in like a lion and goes out like a lamb," brings a hero to match in Jennifer Greene's Mr. March, and Naomi Horton's Slater McCall is indeed a *Dangerous Kind of Man*, coming in April.

Don't let these men get away!

Yours,

Isabel Swift
Senior Editor & Editorial Coordinator

JO ANN ALGERMISSEN
Butterfly

Silhouette Desire

Published by Silhouette Books New York

America's Publisher of Contemporary Romance

SILHOUETTE BOOKS
300 East 42nd St., New York, N.Y. 10017

ISBN: 0-373-05486-6

First Silhouette Books printing March 1989

Printed in the U.S.A.

JO ANN ALGERMISSEN

believes in love, be it romantic love, sibling love, parental love or love of books. She's given and received them all. Ms. Algermissen and her husband of over twenty years live on Kiawah Island in South Carolina with their two children, a weimaraner and three horses. In such beautiful surroundings with such a loving family, she considers herself one lucky lady. Jo Ann Algermissen also writes under the pseudonym Anna Hudson.

One

You don't *have* to get married," Vanessa Monarch's grandfather said. The Colonel, as he was affectionately known by the townspeople of Charleston, puffed on the thin cigar clenched between his teeth, then blew a cloud of blue-gray smoke through his lips. "It's not like you're pregnant."

Vanessa had expected to go over the specials on the evening menu when she'd been summoned from the restaurant on the first floor of the two-story Charleston mansion, to Thaddeus Monarch's second-floor office. She hadn't envisioned discussing her upcoming wedding. Did he think she'd finally set a wedding date because she had to get married?

Vanessa's blue eyes danced merrily as she considered teasing her grandfather. Wisely she resisted the temptation. Her grandfather's sense of humor was severely lacking when it came to her moral conduct. His cigar would be chomped off to the glowing red tip if she dared to announce the birth date of an unborn child.

She watched Thaddeus nervously shift the cigar from one corner of his mouth to the other. For a man who'd come home from World War II with his blue air force uniform dripping with medals, he seemed extraordinarily nervous. It was apparent that he'd felt more at ease with antiaircraft shells popping close enough to smell the smoke from inside the cockpit than talking about her wedding.

"No," Vanessa replied with a grave calmness that befitted the seriousness of the topic, breaking the prolonged silence. "I don't have to get married."

She expected him to settle the roving cigar in the right side of his mouth. He didn't. One of her dark eyebrows winged upward as she wondered if her grandfather planned on conducting a mother-daughter talk concerning her upcoming wedding night. He'd been both mother and father to her since her early childhood, when her parents had drowned in a freak boating accident. Did he think she had reached the age of twenty-six without having learned anything about sex?

Hard as she tried to contain it, a mischievous smile curved her mouth at the thought of the Colonel discussing the birds and the bees with her. Vanessa didn't doubt his courage to broach a territory where other brave men would have trembled—standing outside the ladies' rest-room door while his small granddaughter answered nature's call, for example—but she questioned his valor when it came to openly discussing what would take place in the bedroom between herself and Lee Hayden after they were married.

Once, when she'd been thirteen, he'd introduced the topic. He'd hemmed and hawed, smoked up his office and turned the task over to the counselor at Ashley Hall, the exclusive girls' school she'd attended. Gauging his discomfort from the nervous strumming of his fingers on his desk top and the continual huffing and puffing on the cigar, her smile broadened.

"Lee Hayden was always a good boy. He'll make you happy," the Colonel murmured as though reassuring himself that his only heir would fare well in the care of another man. He slammed his palm down on the desk decisively. Rising, he shot his granddaughter a cocky wink. "I just wanted you to know nothing has to change around here. You don't have to say 'I do.' If you change your mind at the last minute, I'll be there to walk you back up the aisle, head held high. After all, we're Monarchs. You can change your last name to Hayden, but you'll always be my little butterfly."

Vanessa felt her lips tremble, and her eyes shimmered momentarily with a wash of tears. Despite what he'd said, Vanessa knew the Colonel abhorred scandal. Only his profound love for her could have prompted his words.

Touched beyond measure, she slowly circled his antique mahogany desk and put her arms around his shoulders, resting her head on his chest. "I love you, too, Colonel."

Silently she vowed to put aside the reservations she had been feeling over the past month. Prenuptial jitters, she decided. Lee Hayden was a fine man, a pillar of the Charleston community. Her grandfather had little to fear on that score.

Lee would take care of her, but that was just one of her problems. She feared she was giving up the gilded cage of the mansion only to be put behind bars in Lee's condominium. There were times when she felt as though Lee wanted to leave a tape recording for her with detailed instructions on when to breathe in and out.

The Colonel gave her a hearty hug, a rarity between them, then released her when his cigar ash threatened to drop onto the Persian carpet where they stood. He turned to his desk and stubbed out his cigar.

Clearing his throat, he eliminated the rush of emotions that threatened to make his voice quaver. "I know there have been times when you've thought I was being too straitlaced, too judgmental. Maybe even a bit harsh. I just wanted you to know that I'm always here when you need me."

"Hey, you sound as though you're losing a granddaughter," Vanessa chided softly. She kept her disquieting fears to herself. Running to the Colonel with her jitters would only complicate her problems. She was no longer a child. She could solve her problems alone. "What's the old saying? You aren't losing a granddaughter, you're gaining a grandson?"

"Not really," Thaddeus muttered under his breath. "Lee is still pressuring you to stop working at The Butterfly, isn't he?"

"Of course not," Vanessa lied, unable to look her grandfather in the eye.

They both realized Lee's idea of the perfect wife was a woman who managed a household, not a restaurant. Her husband-to-be wanted her to assume her rightful position on Charleston's social register. A banker's wife shouldn't be bartering with the local tradesmen for food and wine, much less deigning to seat her social equals in The Butterfly's dining room.

"I could hire someone to help manage The Butterfly," the Colonel offered reluctantly. "It wouldn't be the same, but I don't want—"

"Nonsense!" Vanessa had no intention of sitting in Lee's condo twiddling her thumbs when she could be useful. "Lee isn't absolutely wild about my continuing to work, I won't deny that. But it's like you said, Lee wants to make me happy. At first he may fuss a bit, but he'll come around."

"You haven't had a fight about your staying on, have you?"

Vanessa breathed a sigh of relief. She didn't have to continue fibbing to her grandfather. She raised her chin and looked him straight in the eye. "No. Lee is too much of a gentleman to fight about anything."

He gives advice and expects everyone to follow it, she could have added, but restrained herself. In her grandfather's present mood, one whisper of doubt from her would have him calling Lee to straighten out her difficulties.

Armed with the knowledge that Lee considered her the ideal choice for a wife, she was capable of fighting her own battles.

She'd been raised with the entire community knowing she was the Colonel's little girl. He'd protectively cocooned her from life's harsh realities. On the rare occasions when he hadn't been around to keep an eagle eye on her, he'd delegated the responsibility to Charles Kimble, The Butterfly's chef. Much to her dislike, it had taken her most of her adult life to convince everyone that they didn't have to walk on tiptoes around her or fear the Colonel's wrath if they offended her.

She certainly wasn't going to let Lee step into her grandfather's wing-tipped shoes at this late date.

"Humph," Thaddeus grumbled. "Sometimes a good rip-roarin' fight clears the air. Remember when I enrolled you in that fancy Swiss finishing school? You blew sky-high! I thought it was where you wanted to go."

Vanessa grinned, remembering the first time she'd gone against her grandfather's wishes. "Yeah," she replied, head nodding. "Only I don't recall you consulting with me to get my opinion. In strict military fashion you handed me change-of-assignment papers and expected me to report to the next field of operations at 0600."

"I wasn't that high-handed," the Colonel rebutted, though his chuckle indicated that he knew he'd probably been worse than depicted. "You really tore into me."

"You deserved it. I could have blindfolded you and put you in front of a firing squad when you said it was my idea. I hadn't even thought of living abroad, much less mentioned it."

Thaddeus shrugged. "Your best friend went."

"Gloria Van Nelson?" Happy to discuss anything other than her wedding, Vanessa waggled her finger in the Colonel's direction. "Gloria was miserable. She married the first man who proposed, before her parents could yea or nay her choice. She knew if she came home her parents would just ship her off again.''

"And divorced her husband within the first year." His brows lowered, then drew together. He watched his granddaughter fold her arms across her chest. "You can relax, Vanessa. I'm not going to start a tirade. Gloria is flaky...."

"Grandfather..." Vanessa warned.

"It's true. I curse the day you chose her as your matron of honor. Heaven only knows what kind of spectacle she'll make of herself at the church."

Flashing her grandfather a cheeky grin that could clearly be read as anticipating Gloria's outrageousness rather than dreading it, she moved toward the door. The Colonel could spend hours trying to change her choice of friends. Sometimes she wondered why he wasted his breath. He knew her loyalty wouldn't waver, even when he used logic. Plain and simple, she enjoyed Gloria's willful pranks. She admired anyone who dared to call their own cadence, march to it and blithely ignore the niceties of Charleston's polite society.

Aware of her grandfather being a stickler for manners, she said, "If you'll excuse me, I have work to do."

"Take the day off. Hell, take the whole week off. I'll handle the suppliers and the staff. I'll shut the front door if things get too hectic for me to handle."

Vanessa wheeled around, and her jaw dropped in surprise. "You're kidding." World peace could be declared, but The Butterfly wouldn't close down to celebrate. The restaurant's doors promptly open at five each evening come peace or war, famine or prosperity.

"You're getting married Saturday," he said by way of explanation. He reached for his humidor and extracted a fresh cigar, then made a shooing motion with his hand. "Go on. Get out of here, child."

Vanessa didn't disobey or countermand the Colonel's order. She had a list a mile long of things she needed to do before the wedding. She'd barely begun to pack her belongings.

Within seconds she was climbing the narrow steps leading to the third story of the antebellum mansion toward the rooms she had played in as a child and had converted into her suite as an adult.

She stopped at the dormer window overlooking the courtyard at the side of the house. She'd miss the giant oak tree with its limbs draped with Spanish moss. Thick, twisted vines of wisteria coiled around the trunk, climbing upward until it disappeared into the green leaves of the oak. Those vines and the azaleas at the foot of the tree had been blooming when Lee had formally asked the Colonel for her hand in marriage.

"A June wedding," she whispered without the eagerness she knew she should be feeling.

She crossed from the window into her room. Her eyes automatically moved to the long white wedding gown hanging on the closet door. Why didn't a thrill of anticipation shiver up her spine? Even Vanessa's most sedate girlfriends had been absolutely giddy during the days before their weddings. Despite her vow to ignore her prewedding jitters, her mind spun with doubts.

She pushed aside the cardboard packing box on her bed and flopped down face forward on her four-poster canopy bed. Rolling to her back, she folded her arms under her head and stared at the white canopy.

"You're being silly," she muttered. "Did you expect to go on being Lee Hayden's girl for the rest of your life? You couldn't procrastinate forever."

Her relationship with Lee had evolved over the years. She'd drifted into becoming known as Lee's girl while he'd attended the Charleston Military Academy. She hadn't consciously made a decision to go steady with Lee; it had just happened.

Sort of like the way we became engaged, she mused.

Lee hadn't officially proposed to her. He'd just taken her acceptance for granted; she wouldn't object after he'd gone through the ritual of asking her grandfather for permission to marry her.

Her eyes momentarily fluttered shut as she tried to imagine Lee sweeping her into a passionate embrace and proposing. She couldn't conjure up an image of that happening. She tried again. This time she tried to picture him on bended knee, which would be more in character for him. Once again, her imagination failed to work. Lee wasn't the type of man who asked for anything. He made decisions and followed through dispassionately.

Unemotional, imperturbable and detached, she thought, summarizing how he behaved toward everyone, herself included. His strengths were her weaknesses. She knew she was prone toward being excitable, caring too much and being occasionally touchy. Like The Butterfly's debit and credit sheet, Lee balanced out her deficiencies.

"But a marriage proposal isn't supposed to be all facts and figures," she muttered. Was that what was bothering her? Had she wanted a passionate avowal of love from Lee? She could whistle Dixie until Saint Peter opened the pearly gates. Lee wouldn't oblige her.

The Colonel would have been delighted to know that Lee hadn't overstepped the bounds of propriety. Lee's style of lovemaking was limited to light kisses and on rare occasions brief fondling. That wasn't to say Lee's kisses weren't pleasant. They merely lacked the fiery passion she'd read about in magazines and novels.

"Romantic drivel," she chided. "Heart-stopping, knock-your-socks-off kisses aren't the foundation for a happily-ever-after marriage."

Talking to herself reminded her of a similar discussion she'd had with Gloria less than a week before. Vanessa had been forced to give monosyllabic replies to Gloria's nosy questions about making love to Lee. Her answers had stemmed from lack of experience, not lack of interest. Vanessa hadn't corrected Gloria's assumption that she'd slept with Lee. Gloria would have been flabbergasted if Vanessa had told her the truth, that she'd never made love with Lee. So she had smiled as though keeping a marvelous secret and given Gloria "yes" and "no" answers.

Gloria, however, told everything. The filter between Gloria's mind and her mouth was definitely missing. Her marriage had abruptly ended due to financial problems, but she had a wealth of sexy stories to tell. When Vanessa had been unable to keep up her end of the conversation with titillating tidbits, Gloria had switched from the let's-trade-secrets tactic to sarcasm.

"Obviously you haven't lost any sleep while sharing Lee's bed. You're both probably snoring before either of you gets undressed."

Vanessa's silence and her grins had brought an ominous warning from Gloria.

"Passion is like the bread maker's yeast," Gloria had said, making her analogy relate to Vanessa's work. "Without it, marriage is flat as a pancake. Tough, too."

At the time the conversation had taken place, Vanessa had laughed and moved the conversation to other subjects.

Vanessa wasn't laughing now.

Gloria's probing had made her contemplate the possibility of a vital ingredient missing in her relationship with Lee. What frightened her was the nagging feeling that the same magical ingredient would be missing in her marriage.

After mulling over the problem in her mind, she'd tried to talk to Lee about it. He'd looked at her as though she had sprouted cauliflower out of both sides of her head. Never one to be at a loss for words, he'd gone into a long spiel about a gentleman respecting a woman. Wasn't that what she wanted?

Vanessa's head made an indentation on the ruffled pillow as she shook her head. She did want respect, but she also wanted passion. Couldn't the two blend, or were they like oil and vinegar? Her fingers plowed through her hair as she struggled with the question.

"Passion and desire can lead to heartache," she reminded herself.

Good Lord, where did that thought come from?

Automatically, she looked toward the hallway. She didn't need to get up to know where her feet would take her. Her thoughts silently took her through her bedroom door down the hall to where Seth Kimble and his father, Charles, had lived before the carriage house above the garage had been renovated. They had had the attic rooms when she'd been a child.

"I don't think Gloria meant that kind of passion," Vanessa said thoughtfully. "Seth and I fought like an alley cat and a junkyard dog the whole time we were growing up. Until..."

Vanessa squeezed her eyes shut. She didn't want to think about that teenage hellion, or the circumstances surrounding his hasty departure from Charleston, or the savage kiss he'd given her before leaving.

Wild child. That's what Seth's father, The Butterfly's chef, had nicknamed his son from the day Seth had arrived on the back steps of the mansion. Her fingers lightly traced over her lips. Seth's kiss had had the flavor of wildness—spicy and hot.

Catching herself in a forbidden daydream, she stiffened her arm and lowered her clenched fist to the coverlet. To this day, she didn't know for certain why Seth had vanished. She'd heard rumors from the twittering teenagers at Ashley Hall about him being caught drunk as a skunk while joyriding in a stolen car, but neither Charles nor the Colonel would confirm or deny the gossip.

Both men had lavished their attention solely on her. At first she'd basked in the limelight. Then, as much as she hated to admit it, within weeks she sorely missed Seth. A tight band of loneliness had circled her heart and squeezed none too gently when she had thought of him.

Time had been the great healer for her heartache. Days, months and, eventually, years passed without hearing a single word from Seth. It wasn't until last month when Charles spotted his picture in Gourmet magazine and showed her the article that she allowed herself to think of him.

Rolling to her side, she picked up her copy of the magazine. It fell open to the page Charles had proudly marked. From the quality of the photograph, she knew a professional photographer had taken it. She scrutinized the stiff pose, trying to find a hint of Seth's devil-may-care grin that had perpetually had him in trouble as a teenager.

"Gone," she whispered with regret, closing the magazine and returning it to the nightstand. "Peter Pan knew he'd grow up if he didn't stay in never-never land. You must have known Seth would eventually grow up, too." Why did it bother her? When they'd been kids, she'd called him every name in the book. Rascal and scoundrel were the polite ones she'd used when adults had been within hearing range. Other names she'd used would have gotten her mouth washed out with lye soap. She should have been glad that he'd changed, grown up into a successful restaurateur.

Licking her lips, she wondered if his kisses had changed, too. Had maturity changed them from spicy to bland? Mentally shaking herself, she heaved herself off the bed and began filling a box with unbreakable knickknacks. Comparing Seth's kisses to Lee's would come next unless she stopped the direction her wayward thoughts were taking her.

"Prewedding jitters is one thing, but disloyalty is another. Lee doesn't deserve that. He's a good man!" Deciding to follow that vein of thought, she continued, "He works hard in his father's bank. He's responsible. He's gentle. We have similar backgrounds—"

The telephone ringing broke into her growing list of Lee's attributes.

"Hi, honey-bunch. How are you doing?"

He's congenial, too, she silently added. "Great. I was just thinking about you."

"Kind thoughts, I assume."

Vanessa squelched the childish impulse to cross her fingers behind her back. She eased her conscience by saying, "Of course. I was just thinking how lucky I am to be marrying a man like you."

"Hold on to that thought because I have some bad news. You know the rumor we've been hearing about the state auditors coming to the bank?"

"Yes."

"I'm afraid it's more than a rumor. A reliable source called Dad this morning. They're going to be here next week."

"Does this mean we'll have to postpone the wedding?" Vanessa twisted the coiled telephone cord around her finger and held her breath.

"Not a chance. We're getting married Saturday if I have to invite the head auditor to be my best man."

Swallowing, Vanessa paused, realizing she didn't know whether she was glad to receive that information or not. Business complications would have been a perfectly acceptable excuse for delaying the wedding.

"The bad news is that I have to break our date for tonight. If we're up for an audit, I want everything in apple pie order."

"Oh."

"Oh?" he repeated. "You don't sound heartbroken."

"I'm not pleased that I won't see you tonight. There were some, uh, last-minute details I wanted to discuss with you—" *like, are you certain we aren't rushing into this marriage* "—but I understand. Usually I'm the one who has to cancel out because of an unexpected busy night here at the restaurant."

"You're a sweetheart. I knew you'd understand. I'm glad you're not the sort of woman who makes a fuss over nothing. Guess that's just one of the reasons you're the perfect woman for me."

Vanessa knew Lee expected her to return the compliment, but she couldn't. Lee did make a fuss when things didn't go as he planned them. Gentlemen seldom made a point by raising their voices, however. Lee would show his displeasure by gradually becoming more distant and withdrawing from her.

"You're sure you don't mind sitting alone tonight? I could call Mother and—"

"No!" The phone cord cut the circulation to the tip of her finger. "I mean, of course I wouldn't mind spending the evening with your mother, but I've a million and one things to do here."

"You're certain you don't mind?"

Sometimes being nice was damned hard. Why couldn't Lee accept her reply? It wasn't as though this was the first time one of them had had to work late. She didn't need his mother to keep her company just because he couldn't be with her.

"I don't mind. Really. You take care of business and I'll help Charles with the food for the wedding reception."

"Boiled water and peanut butter sandwiches?" Lee teased softly, chuckling.

Vanessa grimaced. Teasing her about her lack of culinary skills was like slamming the oven door in the middle of baking a cake—deflating. Lee was one of the few people who knew she could follow a recipe to the ninth degree and still have something mysteriously go wrong between the batter and the finished product.

"I hope no one overheard you," Vanessa said with a tight jaw.

"You know I wouldn't ruin your reputation. The whole town thinks you're responsible for the culinary delights coming from The Butterfly's kitchen, thanks to good old Charles covering for you."

"Let's keep it our little secret, hmm?"

Lee chuckled louder. "Just don't decide to open up your own restaurant and come to the bank for a loan. I'd hate to have to turn down my future bride's loan application."

"No problem. I'm perfectly happy here at The Butterfly." She heard his hand cover the receiver to muffle what he was saying to someone else. "Lee?"

"Sorry. There's a client waiting to see me."

From the change of his tone, Vanessa could tell his client had already entered the office. His mind was no longer on her. "See you. Bye."

She hung up the phone. Her eyes moved to the small crystal butterfly beside it. She remembered finding the exquisite gift sitting in the same spot after she'd had her appendix removed. It had been Seth's get-well gift.

She traced her finger over the fragile wings, then picked up the butterfly and held it up to the light. She could almost hear Seth saying, "See the rainbow colors?"

She returned the crystal to its place with a sigh. Packing her mementos only stirred up old memories that were best forgotten. She'd be better off downstairs helping Charles, she decided, swinging her legs off the bed.

In the ultramodern kitchen downstairs, Vanessa watched Charles nod his approval when the assistant chef, Mickey, ground a dash of nutmeg into the sauce being prepared. His scowl prevented Mickey from pouring sherry into the mixture.

Careless patience had been nonexistent when he'd taught Seth the art of cooking. Charles would bellow, Seth would grimace, she would cover her ears. The years must have mellowed Charles, she deduced as she moved toward the stove.

"Smells wonderful," she commented, smiling.

Mickey beamed. "She-crab soup à la Charles. Wanna taste?"

Shaking his head, Charles stopped Mickey from handing her the spoon he'd been using to stir the creamy mixture. "It's not fit to eat yet. Let it simmer until the crab has reached its peak of flavor."

Charles motioned Vanessa away from the stove to an isolated work area he'd set up to devote to the foods for the wedding. Loaves of sliced homemade bread and small bowls lined the outside edge of the work space. "Sample the fillings for the finger sandwiches."

From having watched Charles prepare food for other large parties, she knew he would alternately layer the mixtures between four slices of bread, then freeze the sandwiches until needed. The day of the event he'd slice them and artfully arrange them on silver trays.

"Peach and mint green?" she said, noticing the color of the fillings perfectly matched the hues in Gloria's bridesmaid dress.

He handed her a set of small tasting spoons. "Everything has to be perfect for your wedding day."

Vanessa dipped the spoon into the first bowl. "Shrimp, sour cream, cream cheese and..." Identifying the ingredients was a game they'd played since she'd been a child. She swallowed before recognizing the elusive spice. "Cayenne pepper?"

"Horseradish."

"Close, huh?"

"No comment."

Changing spoons, she continued the ritual until she reached the last bowl. Charles had begun slicing and dicing a stalk of celery with a French knife. "I'm going to be too chubby to fit into my dress if I keep sampling everything."

"You haven't been eating enough lately to keep a butterfly alive," Charles said disparagingly, giving her slender frame a once-over. He shook his head with regret. "Men like a little meat on the bone."

"I seem to recall your telling Mickey that the closer to the bone the sweeter the meat," Vanessa chided.

She let the spread linger on her tongue before she guessed. "Chicken, chicken soup base, sour cream, white pepper and a kiss of curry."

A tremor coursed through Charles's deft hands, and he came within millimeters of lopping off his thumb. Quickly recovering, he continued dicing, but his eyes nervously shot to the back entrance of the kitchen. "Two out of eight guesses were right. You're improving."

"Expecting someone?" Vanessa asked. She couldn't help noticing how often Charles had glanced toward the rear door.

Charles set down the knife, ducked his head and swiped his hands on the front of his apron.

"I, uh, well..." Charles stammered, obviously searching for the right words. "I hired some extra help... for the wedding preparations."

"Charles?" Vanessa stepped toward Charles when his face blanched, then turned as pink as the peach filling he'd prepared. He must be working too hard, she thought, noticing the dark smudges beneath his eyes for the first time. She became doubly concerned when Charles whipped his tall chef's hat off his head and began twisting it in his hands.

"The Colonel may fire me for doing it."

"Don't be ridiculous," she soothed. She stilled the wringing motions of his hands by placing her fingers around his wrist. "We'd be putting a Closed sign on the front door if it weren't for you. I distinctly remember hearing the Colonel tell you to spare no expense."

Charles shook his head. "You don't understand. I hired—" his eyes evasively darted toward the back door "—someone the Colonel kicked off the premises."

Vanessa saw Charles's eyes widen. At the same time, she heard the screen door squeak. Slowly turning, she followed the direction of Charles's stare. The spoon she'd been holding dropped to the tiled floor, making a metallic clanging noise.

"Seth?" she whispered, her breath catching in her throat.

Time stopped, silence strung between the three of them tautly. Neither Vanessa nor Charles seemed to be able to do anything other than stare at the tall dark-haired, muscular man framed in the doorway.

Vanessa's lungs, starved for oxygen, forced her to inhale deeply. Her head awkwardly jerked back toward Charles. She hadn't conjured Seth up with her wayward thoughts.

Charles had hired his son to help with her wedding feast.

Two

What the hell is he doing here?'' The Colonel's voice boomed from the doorway that connected the main dining room to the kitchen.

Vanessa glanced from her grandfather's angry face to Charles Kimble's deathly white face to Seth Kimble's nonchalant grin. An invisible line separating the owner of The Butterfly from a valued employee seemed to run between the Colonel and Charles, with Charles's foot planted smack dab over the line.

"I wrote Seth and asked him to help with the wedding reception,'' Vanessa responded quietly, willing to take the blame to shield Charles. "It is my wedding.''

Without comment, the Colonel made an abrupt about-face and marched out of the kitchen. Vanessa heard Charles expel his breath, and the ruddy color returned to his face. From behind, she heard Seth's devilish chuckle.

"Still protecting the hired help?" Seth said, lowering his suitcase to the tiled floor.

"You'll have to excuse the Colonel's behavior," Vanessa started, somewhat lost for words to explain his rudeness. "He..."

"Doesn't like surprise attacks?" Seth offered, his voice as neutral as hers.

Vanessa shook her head. Seth's returning home wasn't the enemy attacking the home front. Her blue eyes searched Seth's face for compassion, for understanding. There was none—not where her grandfather was concerned.

"Outflanked?" Seth prompted, lazily widening his smile.

He didn't know why he was purposely antagonizing Vanessa. Maybe it was a defensive reaction to the sinking sensation in the pit of his stomach. Vanessa had changed. He'd expected her to be the same slightly plump teenager he remembered. Instead she'd metamorphosed into a beautiful Monarch butterfly. Or maybe teasing Vanessa until she was absolutely livid continued to be his way of keeping a barrier between them. He didn't know. The only thing he knew for certain was that he wasn't welcome now any more than he had been when the Colonel had run him out of town on a rail years ago.

Two weeks before, he'd received his father's letter via the magazine's publisher. In short order he'd convinced himself that returning to Charleston to make peace with his father was a debt of honor that had to be paid. He sincerely regretted causing Charles nothing but grief and heartache in the past. The least he could do to make amends was to help with Vanessa's wedding.

He owed the Colonel a debt, too. He'd been twelve when he'd arrived at the back door of The Butterfly. The Colonel could have refused to let Charles care for his child on the premises. Later, when he was a royal pain in the ass, the Colonel could have fired his dad. It wasn't until he'd really gotten himself in trouble that the Colonel had stepped in and taken charge.

Seth shoved his hand into his pocket. He'd been at The Butterfly less than five minutes and he knew he'd made his first mistake. He should have cleared his arrival with the Colonel rather than arriving with his baggage in hand. His second mistake centered around his expectations of being heralded into The Butterfly as though he were a conquering hero. The colonel turning his back on him was exactly the reaction he should have expected. After all, he wasn't a long-lost relative. He was a bad penny who'd come back to cause trouble, as far as the Colonel was concerned.

"Seth," Charles murmured, slowly recovering from the shock of seeing his son and the Colonel's reaction. The gap between father and son narrowed. He extended his hand. "I wasn't certain you'd come."

Taking his father's hand, Seth pulled him into his arms for a manly hug. "You knew I'd come," he answered in a fond tone. "All you had to do was ask."

Vanessa stepped backward to avoid letting the emotional reunion between father and son splash over onto her. Why was she feeling left out? Worse, why was she tempted to throw her arms around both men and blubber like a nitwit?

She'd been wrong when she'd studied his picture. Seth had grown older, but he hadn't changed. Beneath the sophisticated tuxedo in the photograph, he was the same arrogant, antagonistic, mean-mouthed...

A wry smile tugged at her mouth. And you haven't changed either, she mused. One minute you want to feel his arms around you, and the next minute you want to scratch his eyes out while you're there.

Charles heartily thumped his son's back, then put him at arm's length. "You've grown."

"A couple of inches—a few pounds here and there. I was so scrawny when I left Charleston that the marines wanted to turn me sideways and use me as a sharpshooter's target," Seth joked. He continued smiling, but the smile didn't reach his eyes. He struggled to keep his gaze on his father when it desperately wanted to linger on Vanessa. And yet he also wanted to observe the pride glowing on his father's face. It was something he'd seldom seen before today. "They didn't think they'd ever make a fighting machine out of me."

Vanessa's eyes followed Charles's hands as they squeezed Seth's biceps and forearms. Yes, she thought, he's lost his teenage lankiness. But the layer of muscles he'd developed didn't account for the natural athletic grace of his gestures. Her thoughts dwindled when Charles's hand gestured toward her.

"What do you think of our little Monarch butterfly?" Charles asked, beaming Vanessa a smile.

"I always was lousy at biology, Dad. I didn't know Monarch butterflies turned into angels."

Seth could have kicked himself when he saw a wild flush tinge Vanessa's cheeks to a rosy pink. Lord have mercy, his hands were trembling just looking at her innocent response. She hadn't learned to hide her reaction behind a mask of gentility.

Vanessa mentally kicked herself for blushing like an Ashley Hall freshman the moment a boy paid her a compliment. She wanted to be as sophisticated as Seth. His glib flattery was definitely something he'd acquired during his absence. She willed the pink tide of embarrassment to subside long enough for her to make a witty comeback.

Too late, she realized, when Charles led his son toward his desk area in one corner of the kitchen.

"Sit down, son," Charles said, removing a stack of papers from the chair beside the desk. He motioned for Vanessa to join them. "It's early, but I'm sure there's a cold beer in the bar's icebox."

"No, thanks, but I'd share a pitcher of ice tea with you, if that's convenient." He settled his hip on a corner of the desk and gestured for Vanessa to take the chair. "I gave up strong spirits while I was in the service."

Intrigued by the silent signals passing between Seth and his father, Vanessa quickly moved to the chair Charles had offered.

"A little wine, maybe?" Charles tested. "This is a special occasion. We ought to have wine to honor it."

Seth chuckled, shaking his head. "I'll go off the wagon long enough to toast the bride with champagne on Saturday. Right now, it would be a dream come true to taste your ice tea. I've been trying to duplicate it in my restaurant. I'm close, but not perfect.

I don't suppose you'd care to share the recipe, would you?"

"I'll reveal my secret ingredient if you'll show me what you added to the icing in that cake featured in *Gourmet* magazine."

"You've got yourself a deal." Seth could have applauded when his dad turned to fetch the tea, leaving him alone with Vanessa. Hungrily his dark eyes devoured her from beneath a fringe of lowered lashes. His heart constricted, then furiously pumped hot blood throughout his system. His fingertips itched to brush back from her face the lock of hair that had fallen forward.

"Overripe raspberries," Vanessa confided in a hushed tone, leaning forward. "I caught Charles grinding the leftover raspberries from the dessert tray in a mortar bowl, then adding them to the tea. He acted like a teenager who'd been caught stealing hubcaps, but he finally confessed."

Seth's spine stiffened as he listened to Vanessa's analogy. The confidence he'd built over the past few years ebbed. What the hell was he doing thinking about touching her? He was the car thief; she was the princess. The Colonel would probably chop off his hands if he thought his precious granddaughter was in danger of being stolen. He wasn't worthy of polishing her shoes, much less framing her face with his hands and kissing her lips.

Dammit, he silently cursed, he'd fallen right into the same self-destructive cycle he'd been in when he left. He still wanted Vanessa; he still couldn't have her. Not then, not now, not in this lifetime, he silently castigated.

Vanessa watched Seth's hand as it repeatedly polished his thigh. Her eyes flew to his mouth. His lips were compressed into a thin straight line. Her mind backtracked, searching for what she'd said that annoyed him.

Tight-lipped, Seth cautioned, "Telling secrets will get you in trouble."

He should have known better than to hope Vanessa hadn't learned the reason for his swift departure from Charleston. The local gossip mongers must have had a field day when the judge had given him a choice between a stiff jail sentence and enlistment in the armed services. Undoubtedly Vanessa had believed every word she'd heard. Nonetheless he didn't need Vanessa to remind him of his past transgressions.

Vanessa recognized the taste of toe jam. She'd put her foot in her mouth by innocently mentioning the word *theft*. Didn't Seth know that she'd never believed the stories she'd heard? Didn't he know that neither Charles nor the Colonel had uttered a syllable to explain the reason behind Seth's departure? Compared to the silence surrounding Seth's name, the recipe Charles secreted was general information available at the public library.

"Seth, I didn't mean to offend you," she apologized. To make amends she reached out to touch the back of his hand. His hand jerked as though she wielded a meat cleaver. Rebuffed, she withdrew hers, letting it fall limply into her lap. "I'm sorry."

Her apology rocked Seth back on his spine. The princess apologizing to the common folk? he mused. That had to be one for the record book. In the past she might have felt ashamed for something she'd said, but nevertheless she would have arched her back, hissed and told him that he was acting out of character. Scoundrels didn't have a sensitive bone in their bodies.

He would have preferred being lambasted. Her contrite apology and the vulnerable exposure of the back of her neck where her hair had parted when she'd bowed her head was reeking havoc on his noble intentions. The urge to drop to his knees and drag her into his arms, kissing that vulnerable spot, accepting her apology came close to overwhelming him.

She's engaged, he reminded himself, erecting a mile-high barrier between his desire and the reality of the situation.

Remaining perched on the desk top was a test of willpower for Seth. He added another stone to the insurmountable barrier between them: class distinction. The Colonel's only granddaughter couldn't hobnob with a lowly private.

Vanessa had learned to govern her tongue, but deep down he knew she was still too blind to see the none-too-subtle lines her grandfather drew between good and evil, right and wrong, employer and employee. She couldn't see them, but Seth knew they existed.

From the corner of his eye, Seth noticed his father balancing a tray filled with a pitcher of ice tea and glasses. Using it as an excuse, he grumbled, "Forget it, princess," and rose to his feet to be of assistance to his father.

"Sit down, son," Charles said, refusing to let Seth take the tray. He handed Vanessa and Seth tall glasses of ice tea, set the tray on his desk and settled into his swivel chair. Leaning back, he took a deep swallow from his glass before asking, "What's your restaurant like?"

"It's glitzy. Mirrors and marble, silver and crystal, and waiters in tuxedos." Seth sipped his tea, watching for his father's reaction. "Nothing like The Butterfly."

"The magazine article said it's the 'in' place for celebrities," Charles added with satisfaction. "We had a few celebrities dine here when they filmed *The North and South*. Several arrived in full costume. I swear, I heard the old mansion sigh when the Confederate officers crossed the threshold. Did you watch the mini-series?"

"I was working." He wasn't, not all those nights. Exiled from Charleston, he knew watching the series would result in an acute case of homesickness. Despite his present predicament, Seth wasn't prone toward masochistic tendencies.

"Too bad. Vanessa had a cameo role." A teasing glint entered Charles's eyes. "You should have seen her...."

Shooting Charles a don't-you-dare-tell-that-story look, Vanessa said, "You're exaggerating, Charles. I had a walk-on part that ended up on the cutting room floor. Seth, tell us what happened in the time between leaving the marines and owning your own restaurant."

"There's nothing much to tell," Seth replied, shrugging off his accomplishments. "Rags-to-riches stories all have the same ingredients: long hours slaving for someone else, being at the right place at the right time, taking a big risk and having it pay off."

"You've tempted the jaded palates of sultans, corporate kings, mingled with the rich and famous," Charles murmured with pride and a touch of envy in his voice.

Seth glanced at Charles. The dreamy expression on his father's face held an unexpected revelation. His father had secret ambitions of running his own restaurant, doing the things his son had done.

As uncomfortable with his father's generous praise as Vanessa had been with his father's exaggeration, Seth started to protest but didn't. Every father wanted to be able to brag about his child. His father had spent most of his years on bent knee, apologizing for him. Seth couldn't deny him the harmless pleasure of elaborating on the truth.

Charles's annotation spurred Vanessa's imagination. From her own experience at The Butterfly, she knew the patrons of a restaurant clamored for the attention of the owner of the establishment. Undoubtedly Seth was included on the guest lists of many of his customers, just as she received invitations to social functions because of her business.

Glitzy, she mused, comparing it favorably against The Butterfly's Southern charm. Equal, but different.

Seth reconsidered how harmless the allusion of easily gained wealth was when he observed the expression on Vanessa's face. He didn't want her to believe he'd left the service and fallen into a cushy bed of roses. He hadn't. He'd worked eighteen-hour days, scrimped and saved, and hocked his soul to cross the line between being a hireling and an owner. The reckless brashness that made him an outcast in Charleston was tailor-made for New York City.

Opportunity hadn't knocked at his door. He'd had to pound the streets looking for a financial backer. Once that formidable feat had been accomplished, he'd had to hustle his butt to buy controlling interest of the restaurant from Sam Jacinto, his partner. Aside from the cash exchanging hands, he'd obligated himself to a gentleman's agreement with his mentor: Once he was established and successful, he promised to investigate the possibility of franchising his New York operation.

Seth grappled with his conflicting emotions, trying to get his priorities back in order. He had two debts of honor to pay back—one from the past—one for the future. He couldn't march forward and simultaneously keep looking over his shoulder.

Let Dad and Vanessa fantasize, he silently decided. He'd always been the one who'd dealt with life's harsh realities. He could control his unruly emotions. By God, he'd keep his hands to himself, help with the wedding preparations and leave before the bride and groom departed from the wedding reception. Scratch one debt from the past, keep your eye on the future, he thought, setting his priorities firmly in his mind.

Lost in introspection, he only caught the last of his father's description. "...six-tier wedding cake."

"Six?" Seth repeated.

"With inverted champagne glasses supporting the tiers," Charles stated, his eyes challenging his son to suggest something more magnificent. To complicate the cake's structural engineering, he added, "And the traditional fruitcake has to be the top layer."

Rashly Seth nodded in agreement. A sharp pain circled his heart as he recalled the custom behind the traditional fruitcake. On their first anniversary, Vanessa and her husband would share pieces of the fruitcake. Adjusting to the idea of Vanessa married to another man was difficult to swallow.

"With your secret whipped-cream icing?" Vanessa requested, further complicating the task.

A sputtering sound came from the intercom system, followed by the Colonel's curt, "Vanessa, telephone—line three."

Excusing herself, Vanessa weaved her way through the maze of kitchen work stations to the telephone mounted near the door.

"Vanessa Monarch speaking." She heard a strangled gasp, then a long pause. "Hello?"

The line went dead. Automatically she clicked the button several times to see if someone had inadvertently disconnected her. Lee might have been calling to inform her of a change of plans. She started to dial the bank's number and stopped. Lee wouldn't have made that queer sound.

"Could have been someone who changed their mind about making reservations," she murmured, returning the phone to the hook. Her shoulders lifted in a small shrug. "Whoever called will probably call back later," she quietly dismissed.

She turned to rejoin Seth and his father but had second thoughts about that, too. Both men were hunkered over Charles's desk, each with a pencil in his hand, making a drawing of her wedding cake. Her heart constricted, and Vanessa placed her hand on her chest.

What was it about seeing Seth that caused those peculiar aches and pains? she wondered. Leftover pangs from her puppy-love days? Vanessa disliked silently admitting to being halfway in love with Seth. At best, realistically, she could only stretch their childhood relationship to the point of armed friendship.

An old hurt she'd buried along with other memories surfaced. Seth hadn't bothered to keep in touch with her.

After he'd left, she'd met the postman at the mailbox, foolishly anticipating a letter from Seth that would contradict what she'd heard at school. He could have written, she thought angrily.

Guilt feelings rushed over her. Friends didn't have to explain their behavior. Just this morning she'd implied that sentiment when the Colonel had verbally maligned Gloria. Nobody was perfect. Of all the people she knew, Lee came the closest to being perfect.

She glanced from Seth back to the phone.

Maybe it was Lee who'd called. Maybe he was experiencing prewedding jitters, too. Maybe...

"I'm going to go see Lee," she whispered, preferring positive action to letting her emotions waffle between Lee and Seth. Face-to-face Lee would see how desperate she was for reassurance and change his plan to work that evening.

Pivoting on one foot, she headed for the front door, calling over her shoulder, "I'm going to take care of the banking."

Years of indoctrination in ladylike behavior enabled her to keep from running. Her mind raced faster than her sedate steps. Saturday she'd marry Lee Hayden. They were perfectly suited for each other. Everyone except Gloria thought he was eminently suitable for her.

Reliable, steady, she mentally argued. He'll be the kind of man who'll be around for a golden wedding anniversary. He'll be dependable, faithful!

Realizing she sounded like a door-to-door salesman pushing mongrel puppies to a recalcitrant buyer, she covered her mouth as though by doing so she'd quiet her thoughts.

Without noticing what she was doing, her stride lengthened and her pace quickened.

Seth Kimble had always been her nemesis. Being a worthy adversary, he'd probably been aware that his arrival would turn her world topsy-turvy—and he undoubtedly loved the prospect. She could almost hear his laughter as she broke into a jog. For two cents, she'd foil whatever underhanded plot he'd devised by handing him a one-way ticket back to New York.

Then her sense of fairness exerted itself. Seth's arrival wasn't the cause of her uncertainty. From the moment she'd drifted into her engagement, she'd privately wondered if complacency rather than love was the adhering factor between Lee and herself.

Thoughts of Seth and his subsequent arrival formed the catalyst that had jarred her from her complacency.

Out of breath, she slowed down as she neared the bank. She patted her hand over her hair in an effort to restore it to some semblance of order. She scanned her casual attire. Knowing Lee's preference for dresses rather than slacks, she wished she'd had the forethought to change clothes before leaving the restaurant. Lee wouldn't appreciate her arriving unexpectedly, especially in a disheveled state.

Chin held high, she pushed on the revolving door. Just this once she expected him to take her as she was, not as he wanted her to be.

She moved to the secretarial desk outside Lee's glass-partitioned office. Joan, Lee's secretary, was only a couple of years older than Vanessa, and a fellow graduate of Ashley Hall. Those facts should have made Vanessa comfortable in her presence, but that wasn't the case. The moment Joan raised her eyes from the loan applications neatly stacked beneath her hand, Vanessa felt out of place and foolish.

"I'd like to speak to Lee, please," Vanessa babbled unnecessarily.

"He's expecting you?"

Squaring her shoulders and drawing herself up to her full five-foot-five-inch height, she lied. "Yes. We spoke earlier."

Joan didn't call her a liar. In fact, Vanessa saw something akin to sympathy in her eyes.

"He's with a customer," Joan replied, glancing over her shoulder at her boss. "I'll buzz through and tell him you've arrived. Won't you have a seat?"

Vanessa felt too antsy to sit, but she knew she'd be less conspicuous in the deep cushions of the chair opposite Lee's office. "Thanks."

She watched Lee through the glass partition window as he picked up the telephone, frowned then glanced in her direction. Her pride demanded that she ignore his facial expression and act as though her dropping by for a chat with the man who'd slipped the diamond engagement ring on her finger was a common occurrence. She cast Lee what she hoped was a dazzling smile.

His scowl deepened; her smile widened.

In her present mood this wasn't the time for him to be standoffish. She needed reassurance, compassion, anything to squelch the impulse to remove her ring and leave it with Joan.

Lee turned his attention back to his customer and gave him the smile she'd silently begged for.

Her eyes traveled to the figure across the desk from Lee. From the expression on the man's face, Lee's cordial smile was worthless. The stranger, who Vanessa guessed was a newcomer to Charleston, looked miserable.

Lee must have refused his loan application, Vanessa surmised.

Her fiancé continued to smile as he pointed to specific items on the application. Refusing the man a loan didn't appear to bother Lee. It bothered her to realize Lee lacked compassion.

Vanessa tried to imagine herself in Lee's shoes. Her fake smile sagged. In similar circumstances, she knew her face would reflect the customer's distress. She had difficulty laying off personnel at the restaurant during the slow months. She'd be an utter failure at informing a man who desperately needed money that he didn't qualify for a loan. Despite the risks, one look at his forlorn expression and she'd be running to the teller, cashing a check on her personal account. Or worse, she'd risk the bank's money. More than likely she'd be fired from Lee's position after the first state audit.

Her attention was drawn back to the scenario unfolding in front of her as Lee rose to his feet. The men shook hands. Lee clapped the customer on the back in a manly fashion. When the stranger walked across the threshold he looked absolutely defeated. Whatever he'd needed the money for, it was damned important to him.

Change your mind, Lee, she silently implored with her eyes. Give him the loan!

"Vanessa," Lee greeted, unobservant of her pleading eyes. "What a pleasant surprise. Come in."

Surprise, yes, Vanessa thought as she gracefully followed him into the privacy of his office, but not a pleasant one. He'd be happier ushering in another loan applicant.

"You didn't give him the loan, did you?" she blurted, knowing better than to ask.

"Sorry, sweetheart. I can't divulge confidential information."

Lee's holier-than-thou air of self-importance irked Vanessa more than his refusal to confide in her. Why hadn't she noticed this facet of his personality before this late date? Because, she silently replied, he's barred you from seeing him at work. Socially, this personality flaw of his came across as self-confidence; professionally, it came across as being callous.

This isn't going to work, she thought silently. Her stomach threatened to revolt as she considered baldly making the statement. Certain Lee was already peeved with her for arriving unannounced, she realized he'd be thoroughly disgusted with her if she disgraced herself all over his desk.

"I'm having second thoughts—"

"Now, Vanessa," Lee soothed, "everyone's nerves are stretched tighter than barbed wire before a big wedding. If I were a selfish man, I'd have insisted on eloping. But I know how important this wingding is for both our families."

"I don't think I'm ready to get married," she stated firmly, but in a small voice. She hated the thought of hurting Lee. They'd been friends long before they'd become engaged. Her hands fluttered restlessly on her lap.

"Of course you aren't ready. I told you that having the reception at The Butterfly would be an enormous undertaking, didn't I?"

"I'm not talking about the reception."

Lee leaned back in his leather desk chair. His hand forged through his crisp blond hair. "I have a feeling we aren't talking about the wedding or the reception. You're upset because you saw me interviewing a loan applicant. You're too kindhearted for this business."

She wasn't feeling kindhearted. Lee's patience and reasonableness made her feel like a spoiled child throwing a tantrum over nothing.

"Come on, honey-bunch, you know I'm a successful banker because I know when to say no. How long would your grandfather have lasted in the restaurant business if he'd given away free meals?"

The idea of the Colonel running a soup kitchen was so farfetched it brought a reluctant smile to her lips.

Lee noted the smile and pressed his advantage. "You wouldn't be happy with an irresponsible man who tossed away your hard-earned money, would you?"

"No, but..." Vanessa refused to be sidetracked. Say it, her conscience demanded. Tell him you think you're both about to make a horrible mistake. But don't hurt him. Her mind swam in a vicious circle as she tried to convey her inner feelings without sounding like a stark raving lunatic. Was it feasible to break the engagement and not hurt him? "Lee, I'm having second thoughts about getting married."

"You're too young?" Lee teased, making light of her fears.

Vanessa grasped for the straw he'd tossed to keep from sinking into the murky waters of confusion. Her eyes leveled with his. "I'm over twenty-one, but there's something I've missed. I'm just not ready to settle down into marriage."

She expected his chin to drop and it did—as he tossed back his head and laughed.

"You're so precious. I guess that's why I love you to distraction. Sweet love, don't look so distraught. Everything is going to be terrific once we're married. Trust me." Lee rose, circled his desk and gave her a swift hug. "You do trust me, don't you?"

"This isn't a matter of trusting you or not," she answered, stubbornly refusing to be treated like a nitwit who didn't know her own mind. She turned her head to the side when he started to brush his mouth over hers. "Lee, where's the fireworks? The brass band? The sexual magnetism?"

Lee settled for kissing her cheek. "Later, love. I promise, you won't be disappointed on our honeymoon. We've waited this long. I want everything to be perfect."

Grasping the front of his suit jacket, Vanessa ardently pleaded, "Don't you understand? I'm not perfect, Lee. I want fire...passion...."

Lee gently patted her hand and pried her fingers from his jacket. He held her hands between his. "Is this the same woman who told me, when she was sixteen, that she wanted a June wedding, with a long white satin dress, and a wedding knight she'd always treasure because she came to her husband pure?"

"I know that's what I said, but I'm not sixteen!"

His hands slid to cup her elbows. Apparently forgiving her for her momentary lapse of sanity, he raised her to her feet and into his arms. "Shh, honey-bunch. You'll have all the fire and passion you can handle Saturday night. We were meant for each other."

Deciding to try humor where emotion had failed, she quipped, "Then take me out tonight or lose me forever."

"I would if I could. I would rather be with you than poring over a stack of delinquent loan accounts." He gave her back an affectionate pat, then curled his forefinger under her chin and raised her head. "Better?"

"A little." Not much, she mutely corrected.

An awkward silence stretched between them until Vanessa felt the muscles in Lee's arms stiffen. Stepping back, Lee straightened his tie, ran his fingers along the cropped hair above his ears and nodded toward the lobby. "Another bank client just arrived. Sorry, honey-bunch, but I've got to put my nose back to the grindstone."

Vanessa glanced over her shoulder. An attractive young woman stood in front of Lee's secretary's desk.

She stared at Lee as though he were her last hope. "Another loan applicant?"

"Jealous?" Lee bantered.

"Should I be?" The thought of Lee messing around with another woman was ludicrous. They'd gone together too many years for her to worry about infidelity.

"Nope. You're the lady in my life."

"She looks anxious to talk to you. I guess I'd better let you get back to work." Vanessa crossed to the threshold of the office. Lowering her voice, she said, "I hope you don't have to turn her down, too. She's near tears."

Lee grinned. "I won't."

"Good."

"If I can't get by The Butterfly tonight, I'll see you tomorrow," he promised.

Vanessa nodded, lingering in the doorway. "We do need to have a heart-to-heart talk."

"Don't worry your pretty little head. Everything's going to be just fine." He picked up the phone and buzzed through to Joan. "Send Charlotte in as soon as Ms. Monarch leaves, please."

Knowing Lee's mind was on his next appointment, she gave him a small wave and moved through the door. She paused next to Joan's desk long enough to say to the woman waiting, "Good luck."

"I'll make my own luck, thank you," the stranger replied stiffly, brushing past Vanessa into the office.

Surprised by the woman's unwarranted hostility, Vanessa glanced from the woman's retreating back to Joan's bland expression. She lifted her eyebrows, silently asking Joan what had brought that on.

"Don't waste your sympathy," Joan advised. "Believe me, Charlotte Bettendorf isn't down and out until the last bell rings."

Deciding she had enough problems of her own without taking on a stranger's cause, Vanessa took Joan's advice. "See you."

Vanessa was in the revolving door when Joan muttered, "Somebody ought to warn her, but it sure as hell isn't going to be me."

Three

Vanessa stood by the rail overlooking Charleston Bay. Fort Sumter could be seen in the distance had she noticed. Sea gulls squawked and strutted, begging for bread crumbs. In other circumstances she would have been amused by their antics. Now, deep in thought, Vanessa was oblivious to anything other than the self-recriminations she heaped on herself. Her fingers rubbed her temple where Lee had dropped a farewell kiss before ushering her from his office.

A sense of failure enveloped her. Lee had pooh-poohed her concerns about getting married. He'd courteously listened to her, but he hadn't really heard anything she'd said.

Oh sure, she mused, he'd promised her anything her little heart desired, including love, passion and undying devotion—commencing on the honeymoon.

She realized she was behaving abnormally. Just arriving at the bank proved that point. And once there, she didn't like what she'd seen.

Lee had neither confirmed nor denied refusing the man's loan application, but the man's facial expression left little doubt in Vanessa's mind as to what had happened. She could learn to accept that as part of Lee's job, but she'd never learn to accept the idea that he thoroughly enjoyed it. She disliked the idea of being married to a man who was capable of refusing someone in desperate need. To her way of thinking, a man could be successful without being callous or coldhearted.

When she'd raised the question of their being sexually compatible, he'd laughed. Not merely grinned or chuckled, she reflected, but he'd given a hearty, knee-slapping laugh!

He wasn't the least bit concerned. Male egotism? she wondered. Wouldn't his ego be deflated if she woke up on their honeymoon and said, "Hey, King's X. There's no fireworks, no clanging bells, no va-va-voom! See you around, honey-bunch."

Either he knows I wouldn't do that or he's confident of his sexual prowess, she deduced. What did he use as a basis for his confidence? They'd always dated or gone steady. He couldn't be any more experienced than she was, could he?

Vanessa mentally shook her head.

"So here I am—a twenty-six-year-old virgin," she muttered, propping her elbows on the rail and framing her face with her hands. "An anachronism. A Southern belle living in the twentieth century. I'm probably the only engaged woman in the world who hasn't been seduced by her intended."

Lee respects you, an imaginary lily-white angel on her shoulder responded silently.

"Whoopee."

She was a good girl in the old-fashioned meaning of the word. Ideologically she had thought remaining a virgin was important. And yet the closer she came to actually marching down the center aisle of the church, the more she'd come to realize that being inexperienced was impractical.

So what was she going to do about it?

Seduce Lee before Saturday?

Vanessa groaned. Lee was unseducable—if there was such a thing. He'd fight for her honor even when she didn't want it. After all, an old-fashioned Southern gentleman protected his Southern belle from his baser instincts. Lee would probably feel guilty if she did manage to seduce him.

"Dreaming about the big day?"

Startled by the unexpected intrusion into her thoughts by a familiar male voice, Vanessa's palm jarred against her jaw and her front teeth nipped her tongue.

"Ouch!"

Aware that he'd sneaked up behind her without being noticed, Seth apologized, "Sorry. I thought you'd hear me coming. Mind if I join you?"

"Pull up a piece of rail and grab yourself some of the view," she replied, gingerly testing her wounded tongue.

Seth leaned against the rail and faced her. "Saturday is the big day, huh?"

"Yeah." She swallowed the sigh that threatened to accompany her monosyllabic response. She couldn't share her inner doubts with Seth. Despite the fact that she'd grown up with him, he was now a stranger.

Seth carefully studied her profile as her eyes blindly gazed toward the water. Her brow puckered and the corners of her mouth turned downward. Something was obviously bothering her.

His protective instincts battled with good common sense. Much as he wanted to comfort her, he didn't trust himself to fold her into his arms. He knew his good intentions would disintegrate like a sugar cube dropped into a glass of boiling water the minute his flesh touched hers.

Patience, he silently coached. Get her talking.

"I noticed some differences in The Butterfly. Dad said you made them."

"Do you like them?" she asked, pleased that he'd mentioned them. She turned toward him to gauge his reaction. In the past his mobile face often gave her clues as to what he was thinking.

Their eyes met, disengaged, then returned.

"I like the changes you've made."

Silently he transposed what he'd verbalized to a personal level. Her dark hair was shorter, curlier than he remembered. Her face had lost its roundness, and her high cheekbones accentuated the almond shape of her eyes. The tiny chicken pox scar was still above her left eyebrow, but it had grown fainter over the years. There were no teenage blemishes marring her smooth, fair skin. *She's exquisitely beautiful.*

He's wildly handsome. Vanessa's thoughts fluttered from The Butterfly to penetrating behind the friendly mask Seth wore to hide who and what he'd become. Physically he'd changed, but his demeanor remained the same. The rough edges had been polished, but he still had the same predatory air about him. Beneath his stylish pastel checked shirt and his pleated trousers lurked a teenager in faded hip-hugging jeans and sweatshirt emblazoned with a disrespectful logo.

"Not too feminine for a restaurant?" she asked, struggling to keep her wits focused on holding up her end of the conversation.

Seth shook his head. "You're giving the customers what they want. A glimpse of what Charleston was before the War Between the States. A time of innocence, when the living was easy: magnolias and mint juleps, candlelight and romance."

Their eyes held. Unconsciously, Vanessa slanted her head to one side as Seth's lowered. She raised on tiptoes; his shoulders bent forward. Her eyes focused on the bow of his lower lip; his watched as her lips parted. In slow motion his hands lifted from his sides as he reached for her slender waist.

Only a breath apart, Vanessa realized that within seconds she'd be kissing Seth Kimble, in broad daylight, within sight of The Butterfly's front steps. She knew kissing Seth would be wrong, but she couldn't move away from him.

Off limits blared through Seth's mind. *She's troubled. You aren't here to complicate her life.* Inwardly he shuddered. He couldn't take advantage of her in a moment of weakness.

His hands dropped to his thighs, and he abruptly turned to the railing and grabbed hold with both hands until his knuckles turned white.

An overwhelming sense of loss invaded Vanessa. Disappointment blossomed into self-doubt. Was there something about her that turned men off? Lee wasn't eager for her kisses, and Seth had blatantly rejected her. Why?

"Seth?"

"For heaven's sake, Vanessa, you're marrying someone else Saturday. You'd be mad as hell if I kissed you."

Later, maybe, Vanessa thought, but not now. Her mouth felt dry, her throat tight. She wanted his kiss. A flash fire of guilt and embarrassment reddened her cheeks. Disguising her wounded pride behind a mask of anger, she replied, "I'd slap you silly, you presumptuous . . ."

"Scoundrel?" Seth supplied when she stopped short of hurling a disparaging name at him.

"Worse."

"Lout?"

"Much worse."

Seth tossed his head back and laughed. "Rumpelstiltskin?"

She grinned, remembering how often he'd goaded her into calling him unspeakable names and then blackmailed her into joining him in some outrageous escapade by threatening to tattle to her grandfather.

Quick on the uptake, she sniped good-naturedly, "You have more hairy warts than Rumpelstiltskin."

A devilish glint lit his dark eyes. "How do you know about my wart? Shame on you, princess. You've been peeking—a peeking princess. Tsk, tsk, tsk!"

"You don't have any warts," she retorted impudently to shut him up. The look on Seth's face was priceless. Of course, she didn't know whether or not he had warts, but Seth obviously didn't know that fact.

"Why you little—"

"Careful," she warned, winking at him as though she had intimate knowledge of his physique. "I could send those Polaroid pictures to one of those racy women's magazines."

Seth hooked his thumbs on the slender belt circling his waist. "Go ahead. Haven't you heard the motto It Pays to Advertise. Just imagine the sorts of fan mail I'd get. After being with you less than ten minutes, I could use an ego booster."

"I could use one myself," Vanessa blurted truthfully. Reflexively her hand clamped over her mouth. She hadn't meant to say that.

"I beg your pardon?"

"Nothing." She whirled around and started toward home.

Seth reached out, grabbed her upper arm and swung her back around. "From what Dad says, Lee Hayden is one of Charleston's finest, at the top of the most eligible bachelor list. Why the hell would you need an ego booster? He isn't mistreating you, is he?"

Caught off balance, she collided with his chest. His heart pounded in her ear and his masculine cologne tingled her nose. She craved to be held closer, tighter. Realizing she was a hair's breadth away from making a complete fool of herself, she dryly said, "You're the one who's going to leave me with bruises."

He loosened his hold, letting his fingers slide down to her wrist until they made a ring around her wrist. His face blanched white when he saw the red marks on her arm.

"I'm sorry," he said hoarsely.

Recovering her equilibrium along with her sanity, Vanessa appreciated both his willingness to come to her rescue and his abject contriteness.

"You didn't hurt me."

Someone has, Seth thought, hanging on to her wrist with tenacity. Persistence was the key to his success. He knew she'd eventually tell him what was bothering her. "Then what's the real reason you need an ego booster?"

"Would you let go if I told you my personal problems aren't any of your business?" She felt his manacle grip tighten on her wrist, silently communicating his reply.

She couldn't reveal the doubts she had about marrying Lee without being disloyal. Seth hadn't been around. He wouldn't understand how she'd drifted along in a relationship until she found herself at the brink of getting married. Seth was a physical man. He wouldn't understand how Lee had been able to control his physical urges.

From the look she'd seen in Seth's eyes when he thought Lee had mistreated her, she knew uttering one wrong word would precipitously end the wedding plans: Lee would be hospitalized.

As though he'd been reading her mind, Seth encouraged her to let him help by saying, "Sometimes

it's easier to tell your problems to a stranger, or someone who hasn't been around for a while.''

A hypothetical situation was the solution, Vanessa
decided. Let Seth think she was worried about one of
her friends, someone they both knew.

"Gloria," she murmured. "You remember Gloria
Van Nelson, don't you?"

"Your girlfriend from Ashley Hall?" He watched
Vanessa's head bob up and down. "What does she
have to do with your wedding?"

"Not my wedding," she fibbed, putting Gloria into
her size-seven shoes. *Forgive me, Gloria,* she silently
apologized in advance. "I'm worried about Gloria
getting remarried."

"Remarried?" Remembering what a flaky teenager Gloria had been, his shock stemmed from his
surprise at Gloria catching one unsuspecting male,
much less two.

"She divorced the man she met and married after a
five-day whirlwind courtship. Now she's drifted back
to her old high school sweetheart and they're planning on getting married next month."

Seth watched Vanessa's blue eyes skitter from the
bay to the shady park adjacent to the water. She was
looking everywhere other than meeting his eyes. He
listened carefully, reading between the lines of what
Vanessa said. Lying was a difficult chore for Vanessa.
She stammered and stuttered each time Gloria's name
passed through her lips. Was she substituting Gloria's
name for her own? he wondered.

"I'm not certain, uh, Gloria loves Pete."

"Why?"

"Oh, no particular reason...just things that I sense are missing in their relationship."

"Such as?"

Vanessa grimaced. Gloria would kill her if she could hear the web of lies Vanessa was stringing together. "Pete isn't very, uh, you know."

"Affectionate?"

"No. That's not exactly what I mean. He's caring. He hugs and kisses her. I just don't think they..."

"Make love?"

Vanessa's long, sooty lashes blinked over her troubled eyes. "Yeah. I think they're better friends than lovers."

"You think a man and woman who are engaged should find out if they're sexually compatible?" He tried to keep the incredulous note out of his voice, but he knew he hadn't when he witnessed Vanessa's teeth sinking into her lower lip.

Good Lord, Vanessa silently moaned. I'm giving him the impression I think women should sleep around before marriage. She had to correct that misconception.

"G-G-Gloria's been married before. It would be different if she was a..." Vanessa felt herself getting deeper into a hole. Her initial effort to make Seth think she was sophisticated had been blown sky-high.

"A virgin?"

Vanessa forced a strained burst of laughter from her throat to lead Seth away from the truth. "Gloria is my age. Pete wouldn't expect her to be a virgin even if she hadn't been married."

The mixed signals Vanessa had tried to send were wasted on Seth. She'd changed the names to protect her innocence, but he knew Gloria and Pete were really Vanessa and her future husband. The news that Vanessa's virginity was intact amazed, dismayed and pleased him.

In his mind, Vanessa had every reason to be worried. Any man who'd dated her for years, who was engaged to marry her and hadn't managed to sleep with her, had to have a subzero sex drive!

"Sounds to me like something is drastically wrong with Pete," he rejoined, careful to continue using the fictional names. "You have good reason to worry about, uh, Gloria. Most women want their first home to be designed without a kitchen. It sounds like Gloria will need to find a place without a master bedroom!"

Genuine laughter bubbled through Vanessa's lips. His subtle inference that Lee did not conform to society's expectations was ludicrous. "No, I don't think that's their problem."

"You're certain?" Had he misconstrued something Vanessa had said? he wondered. She sounded absolutely certain "Pete" was normal. Maybe she *was* talking about two of her friends and not her own problem.

"Well, I haven't slept with Pete, but I'd bet he's straight. Pete respects Gloria," Vanessa explained, stating the reason Lee had given. "He's the perfect example of a real old-fashioned Southern gentleman."

"I guess there are some advantages to being a rogue," Seth murmured as he pictured the wedding night with the bridegroom fumbling around, unable to please his new wife. "Unless I'm badly mistaken,

I'd say Gloria's second marriage isn't going to last as long as her first one.''

Vanessa's doubts intensified after hearing Seth's dire prediction. Inwardly cringing, she asked in a hushed voice, "You don't think Gloria should marry Pete?"

Caught in the dilemma between telling Vanessa to head for the nearest motel with her fiancé and not wanting to think about her sharing a bed with another man, his mind raced to find a means to artfully dodge her underlying question: *Should I marry a man I haven't slept with?*

She wanted an unbiased opinion. He sure as hell couldn't give her one.

"I think Pete's damned lucky to be marrying a divorcée."

"But what if Gloria hadn't been married?" Vanessa glued her eyes to the lapping water below the concrete wall and prayed she wouldn't blush. "Hypothetically, I mean."

Ill at ease, Seth shifted from one foot to the other as he soundly cursed himself for initiating the conversation. He was the last person who should give her advice. To his recollection, he hadn't crossed paths with a virginal woman in the past six years, much less been put in a position where he'd been asked to voice his opinion. He didn't know a damned thing about whether or not a platonic relationship could evolve into marital bliss. The only advice she'd get from him would have the same value as a Confederate dollar— zilch.

"Hypothetically?" he repeated, lengthening the pause, pretending his five-cent vocabulary wasn't up to her ten-dollar word.

"Don't pull that you're-smarter-than-I-am routine on me," she scolded. "You used to do that when we were kids."

Sidetracking her, he joked, "You were smarter. I've got the report cards to prove it."

"Book learning isn't helping me solve Gloria's problem," Vanessa countered, slowly raising her eyes from the water until they met Seth's.

"You're a helluva lot smarter than I am. I can't solve Gloria's problem," he said honestly. "I'd just make it worse."

A capricious gust of wind whipped off the bay, ruffling Seth's dark forelock until it settled on his forehead. Vanessa restrained from brushing it back into place. She wanted to touch him, to reassure him that his opinion had always meant a great deal to her.

Academically she had pulled better grades than Seth, but he'd been people-smart, street-smart. Nobody took advantage of Seth Kimble without facing the consequences, and he'd made certain no one took advantage of her soft heart, either.

She tucked her hand in the crook of his arm and rejoined, "You were here when I needed you. Welcome home, Seth. I'm glad you're here."

Seth's fingers closed over her slender hand. He wanted to raise her palm to his lips and kiss it, then slowly curl her fingers over his kiss for safekeeping. He'd lacked the wisdom to give her the answers she needed, but he had a few questions of his own regarding Lee Hayden, her future husband, that he planned on investigating.

"I'm glad to be here." He shortened the length of his natural gait to match hers. "I'll walk you back to

The Butterfly, then I have a few old acquaintances I want to look up."

A half an hour later, after one of the tellers at the bank had told Seth that Lee usually stopped off at the Do-Come-Inn before he went home, Seth unhurriedly strolled into the bar. He'd been in similar bars, but it wasn't the type of place he expected to find a banker.

Sleazy, he silently surmised, letting his eyes adjust to the filtered light coming through the smoke-glazed front window. Few customers would notice the Grade B sticker from the Charleston Health Department that was partially hidden by a scraggly potted plant, but Seth did. Substandard adherence to the health regulations had earned the establishment its undesirable rating.

A rotund barmaid, dressed in a calico-print shift that had seen better days, approached him. She tossed a dingy bar towel over her shoulder, flounced her curly blond hair with one hand and gave Seth an unrestricted view of her ample breasts. "My name's Sheila. What'll it be, mister?"

"A draft beer."

Inconspicuously he scanned the room, stopping when he spied a blond-haired man dressed in a three-piece suit sitting in a back booth. In a blue-collar working man's bar, Lee Hayden's navy blue suit stuck out like a Yankee's uniform in a Confederate camp.

The back of the booth prevented Seth from seeing Lee's companion, but he could see that Vanessa's fiancé was holding someone's hand—someone whose fingertips were painted a dusky pink.

Fury boiled through Seth. He wanted to jerk Lee out of the booth and pound some sense into his head. Lee was supposed to be marrying Vanessa Saturday. What the hell was he doing holding another woman's hand, smiling as though the woman across from him would soon be his bride?

"Here you go, stranger," the barmaid said, sliding a frothy beer between his hands. "Wanna run a tab?"

Seth nodded, too angry to speak through the knot lodged in his throat. His eyes swung to the woman who'd begun to amiably chat with him.

"Business is slow," she commented. "Just the regulars. You'd think during the tourist season we'd be packed, huh?"

"Yeah," Seth grunted as he visualized several less-than-charming methods of tearing Lee Hayden limb from limb.

One thought kept Seth from taking action: Vanessa's reputation. A single jab to Lee's solar plexus would result in Vanessa being subjected to the waggling tongues of the gossips. They'd love nothing better than to maliciously whisper the gory detail of who had landed the punch and why.

Why hadn't those same gossips informed Vanessa of Lee's extracurricular activities? he wondered. Lee being a banker who controlled half the loans in town could be one reason, Vanessa being one of the most well liked women in town could be another. Nobody, himself included, wanted to break the bad news to her.

"...horse-drawn carts in this part of town." The barmaid finished her list of ideas that would draw tourists out of the Straw Market area to the south side of town. She eyed Seth's hands. He clutched the pilsner glass, but he hadn't taken a drink. "Something wrong with the beer?"

"No." He jerked his head toward the back booth. His drawl became more pronounced when he said, "Guess you don't get many yuppies like him in here, huh?"

"Mr. Hayden?" Her hand automatically removed the bar towel she'd flung over one shoulder, and she began swiping the dried rings on the top of the bar. "You've heard the old saying, 'You can't tell a man by the cut of his clothes?' Well, don't be fooled by his pin-striped suit."

He wanted to ask the name of Lee's companion, but he knew better than to appear too nosy. Nothing could shut the mouth of a friendly barkeeper quicker than a stranger asking too many questions about a regular customer.

Seth downed a swallow of beer. Cold but bitter, he thought, remembering a time when he'd preferred the flavor of beer over raspberry tea. He wiped off the foam clinging to his lips with the back of his hand.

"Looks like a carpetbagger to me," he commented nonchalantly, sealing a common ground between himself and the barmaid as he slouched forward to form a visual barricade between the woman and Lee. It was okay for a Southerner to be poor because of circumstances beyond his control, but it wasn't okay to be a Northerner under any circumstances.

"Copperhead," Sheila retorted quietly. "The Haydens helped the Yanks after the war. Copperheads are worse than carpetbaggers. You think they're on your side, but behind your back they're kissin' the rumps of the enemy. By now, I reckon the Hayden family owns half of Charleston county 'cause of foreclosures. When you borrow money from the Haydens' bank, you take your shirt and a pint of blood in for collateral.''

Seth glanced over his shoulder, taking a second look for Sheila's benefit. ''His wife's a looker.''

Sheila giggled, covering her hand with her mouth to stifle the snorting noises. ''Wife, hell. Hayden's engaged to one of the sweetest little gals in Charleston from what I heard—her grandpa owns that fancy restaurant, The Butterfly.''

''Oh, yeah? She must have a few coins. How come she lets Hayden run around on her?''

''Don't know, I reckon.''

''Somebody ought to tell her.''

Sheila shrugged her broad shoulders. ''What Miss Monarch don't know won't hurt her. Why two good women would fall for that bastard is beyond me. Charlotte Bettendorf ain't rich, but she's too good for the likes of him.'' Picking up his glass, Sheila asked in a louder voice, ''You want a new head on this one?''

Seth could see from the muscle nervously ticking beside Sheila's right eye that she'd said more than she should have. He raised his hand to keep her from refilling his glass, pulled a couple of dollars from his pocket and tossed them on the bar.

''Guess I'm not too thirsty after all. Keep the change, Sheila.''

''Y'all come back, ya hear?''

Casually waving, Seth crossed the narrow width of the bar and opened the door. As he started to close it, the woman who'd been seated with Lee Hayden stood and moved to the bar. She carried a tray in her hands and wore a frilly apron.

Seth's eyebrows shot upward. Lee's girlfriend worked at the Do-Come-Inn? Not wanting to draw attention to himself, he shut the door and started down the sidewalk.

That explains everything, he mused. Sheila's kind remarks about Lee's girlfriend... Vanessa's problem... Lee's choice of who he wanted to marry and why he hadn't pushed Vanessa sexually.

A banker from a prominent Charleston family would be slitting his social throat if he married a waitress from a low-class ginny joint. Lee was playing it smart. He'd have Vanessa, and a girlfriend on the side.

More than anything, Seth wanted to rectify that situation by grinding Lee Hayden's handsome face into the concrete sidewalk. At all costs he had to control his hot temper. Lee Hayden was a respected member of the community; Seth Kimble had a bad reputation. He'd get a great deal of physical satisfaction by beating the daylights out of Lee, but his fists wouldn't solve the problem. Lee would get sympathy, and Seth would get kicked out of town. Brute force wasn't the solution.

Lee was smart, so Seth would have to be smarter.

"You can count on one thing, Mr. Fancy-Pants Hayden," Seth grumbled as he moseyed back toward The Butterfly. "You aren't getting married to Vanessa on Saturday. You can count on that like the greenbacks in your damned bank."

Four

___

For lunch?'' Vanessa repeated the time of Lee's invitation. He knew that on Wednesdays she scheduled herself in to work as The Butterfly's hostess. Wednesday evenings she was off work. To complicate matters, Seth was standing within a foot of the phone and wasn't making any pretext about not eavesdropping. "Dinner would be a better time."

"Can't. The trials for last quarter's savings accounts don't balance. Dad and I are staying late to see if one of the tellers transposed some figures."

"Lee, you promised—"

"We'd get together today. So? What's more important to you? Letting the customers seat themselves or having lunch with me?"

"What's more important to you?" she countered,

her voice firm. "Having dinner with me or balancing your infernal books?"

"You're the one who wants to talk about the wedding Saturday. As far as I'm concerned, everything is set."

"You're being unreasonable."

Totally disregarding her need for privacy, Seth mouthed, "Trouble?"

Vanessa motioned with her hand for him to go away, then covered her ear when Seth started to say something. Why couldn't the blasted man do the polite thing and at least pretend not to be all ears?

"I love it when you make wife-type noises." Lee chuckled. "Gabriel's. Twelve o'clock sharp."

Seth watched Vanessa lower the phone back to its cradle. He was fairly sure that she badly wanted to slam down the receiver, but she controlled her temper for his benefit. From what he'd overheard, he gathered Vanessa wanted to talk to Lee, but not over lunch.

After getting less than two hours' sleep the previous night, his mood was as dark and heavy as the nimbus clouds outside. He'd noted the smudges under Vanessa's eyes, too. Both of their tempers were on a short fuse. Seth decided her being out of sorts wouldn't help Lee's cause. He lit the wick on her temper by saying, "No 'I love you, darling' before you hang up?"

"Shush," Vanessa snapped. Her head pounded beneath her fingers as she massaged her forehead. When she hadn't been worrying about how to call off the wedding and managed to catch a few winks of sleep, she'd had vivid dreams of the man who'd taken great delight in listening to her private conversation. "I don't suppose I could talk you into being the host during lunch, could I?"

"Sorry. I've made plans." He hadn't, but he knew how to set Vanessa's teeth on edge during her lunch with Lee. "Yesterday you were so concerned about Gloria that I decided to call her and invite her to lunch."

"You what!" A fresh charge of pain shot from the base of her neck through her skull as her head jerked upward. She couldn't let Seth have a heart-to-heart talk with Gloria without warning Gloria first. Once Gloria told him that she'd been living with Pete for months, Vanessa would have to answer a whole gang of embarrassing questions.

"Well, I haven't called her, yet."

"I don't think taking Gloria to lunch is a good idea." She knew he'd ask why and she tried to think of a rational answer, but her head felt like a bowl of stale grits.

"Why? Pete isn't the jealous type, is he?"

Vanessa could have kissed Seth for giving her the answer to his own question. She started to nod, then stopped, knowing her head would explode with any fervent gesture. "Yes. Pete's insanely jealous."

"From what you said, I had Pete pictured as a passive kind of guy. Passionless." Seth inwardly grinned. Any element of doubt he'd had that Gloria and Pete were the ones with the problems disappeared. Vanessa had been confiding in him about her own problem. Now she was scared to death he'd get to Gloria before she did. Mercifully he let her off the hook. "I told you I had a knack for making trouble even when my intentions were pure. I guess I'd better let you

handle Gloria's problem. And, since I'm in a benev-
olent mood, I'll take over your lunch duties, too."

Relief flooded over Vanessa. Without thought she
flung her arms around Seth and gave him a big hug.
Seth reflexively returned her affectionate gesture.

Neither of them heard the approaching footsteps or
smelled the aroma of cigar smoke.

"I beg your pardon, but this happens to be a place
of business," the Colonel interrupted, "not the tun-
nel of love."

Vanessa's heart skipped a beat when she heard the
Colonel's tone. She knew he'd drawn the wrong con-
clusion.

"I was thanking Seth for—"

"Shut up," Seth whispered, increasing the pressure
of his hands around her waist. He knew the Colonel
would accept only the military response: *No excuse,
sir.*

The Colonel removed his cigar from his mouth, exhaled a cloud of smoke and pointed the red tip toward Seth. "If you'd be so kind as to release my
granddaughter..."

From the look in the Colonel's eye, Seth realized
Vanessa's grandfather was recalling the circumstances when he'd spoken similar words. It had been
the night Seth had departed from Charleston. Injustice and social discrimination had broadened his streak
of rebelliousness and given him the courage to dare to
enter the Colonel's office to look for Vanessa. For one
brief moment, he'd unleashed the pent-up passion
he'd closely guarded. She'd been napping on the
leather sofa, half-asleep, when he'd soundly kissed
her. The memory of her sleepy response, her lips

clinging as her body arched up to meet him, had carried him through marine boot camp. Unfortunately, the Colonel must have been right on his heels when he'd entered his office. The words he'd just heard were nothing to compare with the questions the Colonel had asked after he'd ordered Vanessa from the room.

Seth's square jaw jutted forward aggressively as he dropped his arms and stepped backward. Then, as now, he'd been innocent of the charges the Colonel leveled against him. Then, as now, he couldn't speak his piece. Some debts had to be repaid with silence.

"Excuse me, sir, I have to start designing Vanessa's wedding cake."

Vanessa impaled her grandfather with an icy glare. Seth had always been in the wrong, according to the Colonel's strict code of behavior. This was one time she was going to set the record straight.

"You acted like he'd attacked me! Couldn't you see that I hugged him, not the other way around?" The disbelief that she read on her grandfather's face exasperated her. Once he'd made up his mind, he couldn't be swayed. She knew how intractable he could be, but her stubborn sense of fairness made her add, "Seth was kind enough to volunteer to do my job here while I met Lee for lunch. My hugging him was how I expressed my appreciation."

"You don't impulsively embrace a man. Seth isn't a boy, Vanessa," the Colonel warned, ignoring her explanation. "You could tease him when you were both kids, but a lady doesn't tease a man."

The authoritative tone in his voice was familiar, but there was something in her grandfather's eyes that she'd never seen. She'd recognize love or anger or censorship. But this look was different. Was it pity? Who did he pity? Seth? Herself? She stepped closer, intrigued. No, she decided, it wasn't pity. Fear? she silently guessed. Did the Colonel fear Seth? Why? Even in the most trying circumstances Seth had always treated the Colonel with respect.

"Why don't you like Seth?" she asked candidly.

"He's dangerous."

"How?"

"Never mind how. You mark my words. He'll cause trouble."

"Grandfather, that's ridiculous," Vanessa protested. "Seth came here to help with the reception, to see his father. You're treating him like a sixteen-year-old hoodlum!"

"Stop defending him. Don't you realize the man is in love with you?"

Vanessa shook her head. Dryly she replied, "Now we both know where I get my vivid imagination from, don't we?"

"Imagination, hell. I heard him say it with my own ears."

"When?"

"When he invaded my office without permission, before he left Charleston. You can stop shaking your head, missy. I know you're thinking that he's changed. He hasn't. His kind never changes. I've known men like Seth Kimble. Wild. Untamable. A loner."

His eyes skirted away from her, hiding something.

There was more to Seth's leaving than she had heard, she was certain of it. "Did you have something to do with Seth leaving Charleston?" she asked.

"Yes and no."

For a second, when her grandfather's military carriage slipped and his cigar dangled lifelessly from the side of his mouth, Vanessa had a glimpse of a man older, wearier, than the man who'd raised her.

"I asked similar questions after Seth left. You told me I was too young to understand. I'm twenty-six, Colonel. I want to know the truth."

A dry choking sound passed through her grandfather's lips. It could have been a cough or a gasp of pain. Vanessa swiftly moved to his side.

"Don't fuss." He sidetracked Vanessa with his faked coughing seizure long enough to gather his wits. "Seth and a buddy of his went joyriding and got caught by the police."

"Was Seth driving the stolen car?"

"What difference does it make as to who was driving? Being a thief or an accomplice doesn't make him innocent."

"Didn't anyone bother to ask?"

"We all asked...Charles, the judge, me. Seth clammed up tighter than a cherry stone clam."

"He didn't have a previous record, did he? Why didn't the judge parole him to his father's custody?"

"Because, missy, Seth's stick-it-in-your-ear attitude didn't win friends or influence the judge. He was damned lucky that Charles and I convinced the judge not to hang him from the highest oak tree. As a special favor to me, the judge agreed to let Seth join the military service."

"What happened to Seth's friend?"

"He didn't go to jail, if that's what you're worried about."

"What branch of the service did Seth's buddy join?" Vanessa asked. Watching her grandfather roll the unlit cigar butt between his fingers, she was convinced he'd told her part of the truth, but not all of it.

"His parents shipped him off to college."

"To college? What kind of justice is that?" How could the judge force Seth to join the service and sentence the other boy to fraternity life? She was beginning to understand why Seth hadn't kept in contact with any of them.

The Colonel started to speak, then clamped his lips shut.

There was more, Vanessa deduced. Something else her grandfather wasn't particularly proud of.

"There's something you aren't telling me. Why? Who are you protecting—me or yourself?"

The Colonel reached into his pocket and extracted a Zippo lighter with the U.S. Air Force seal encrusted on top of stainless steel. One flick of his thumb and a flame leaped to the charred end of his cigar. "I'm not at liberty to divulge anything else."

Dissatisfied, Vanessa said, "I'll ask Seth what happened."

The Colonel stonewalled her, dragging on his cigar, blanketing a blue-gray barrier of smoke between them. "Some secrets are better off buried in the past," was his ominous warning as he turned, heading up the steps to his office.

From the entry of the restaurant, Seth's dour expression changed to one of glee as he watched Vanessa wield her LeBaron convertible out of the parking lot as though it were an underpowered tank. If her driving accurately indicated her mood, Lee was in for trouble with a capital *T*.

He'd been smarting from the invisible whip the Colonel held over him. Keeping a civil tongue in his head had been difficult. Each time he felt on equal footing with Vanessa, the Colonel appeared, pushing him back into the quicksand of his insecurities. Sooner or later, he and the old man would have to settle their ancient disputes.

Two hours later Seth thought he'd made it through the lunch trade without anyone recognizing him, until he heard an unfamiliar voice speak his name.

"Aren't you Seth Kimble?" inquired a blonde wearing enough makeup to make a Barnum and Bailey clown jealous. Four-inch earrings swayed coyly, kissing her bare shoulders, inviting male eyes to dip lower to enjoy the hint of cleavage exposed at the V of her peacock-blue dress.

"Gloria?"

Of Vanessa's friends who attended Ashley Hall, only Gloria was bold enough to wear such dramatic attire and still appear attractive. When the other girls, including Vanessa, tried to copy Gloria's style, they looked like adolescents imitating high-priced call girls.

Seth noticed the guileless smirk on her face. It didn't take a genius to know Vanessa had talked to Gloria prior to her arrival at The Butterfly.

"Join me, won't you?" she invited. Her long red-lacquered nails patted the cushion of the seat beside her.

"I'm playing host...."

"Everyone knows the restaurant closes at two-thirty. I purposely waited until everyone had left before speaking to you. Please, sit."

Accepting her invitation, Seth twirled the high-back chair around and straddled the seat. This close, the fragrance of her musky perfume enveloped him. A weaker man would have moved closer, seeking the source of the perfume. Seth crossed his arms on the back of the chair and propped his chin on the back of his hands, waiting for Gloria's next move.

"Vanessa tells me that my ears should have been burning yesterday." Her neatly plucked eyebrow arched. "Why can't I visualize you as someone who'd be giving advice to the lovelorn?"

"Probably because we didn't grow up under the same roof," Seth replied, reaching toward the silver bowl in the center of the table and popping an after-dinner mint into his mouth.

Gloria purred, "Enchanting idea."

"Vanessa mentioned that your flirting days are numbered," Seth succinctly replied, discouraging her from practicing her womanly wiles on him, and encouraging her to shoot straight.

Under another set of circumstances, Seth knew he would have responded differently. Gloria had been around the world and sampled a variety of forbidden fruit. Nothing he could say or do would shock her. Typically Gloria was exactly the type of woman that made his spatula quiver.

But here in Charleston, underneath the roof of The Butterfly, the circumstances were different. Vanessa and only Vanessa occupied his every thought, his every movement. In both thought and deed, he was totally unlike Lee Hayden.

Gloria waved a one-carat diamond under Seth's nose. "You're referring to this?"

"And the fact that you're Vanessa's best friend."

Smiling, Gloria quipped outrageously, "Best girlfriends always share good things."

"Girls, yes. Women, no."

Gloria leaned back against the brocade cushion, fully aware of the impact her bust line would have.

The final test, Seth mused, failing miserably by keeping his eyes on her face.

Gloria relaxed from her pose and tugged down the hemline of her short dress. A genuine smile curved her lips and crinkled lines beside her eyes. The contralto pitch of her voice raised to its normal soprano range as she confided, "Everybody but Vanessa thought I was a certifiable twit back in high school. Dumb blondes were in fashion. So were Jimmy Dean-type boys."

"There was one major difference between your acting like a dumb blonde and my giving the impression that I didn't give a damn about anything."

"You don't have to tell me. You *didn't* give a damn." She traced a droplet down her water goblet. "With one exception."

Seth conceded her point by nodding his head. They both knew without saying who that exception was: Vanessa Monarch.

"Aside from your kiss-my-butt attitude, do you know what I remember about you . . . before the scandal?"

"What?"

"Big, hungry eyes," she replied without the least hint of seductiveness. Flattery wasn't her objective; curiosity had prompted her sincere observation. "Tell me, Seth, now that you've been outside of provincial Charleston, did you find someone to satisfy your yearning?"

"No."

He could have elaborated. For some unknown reason he felt a peculiar sort of kinship to Gloria. He sensed that she'd left Charleston with hungry eyes, too, seeking someone or something to fill the void within her. Neither of them had succeeded, not on a personal level where it counted.

"I thought I had." Her eyes filled with pain as they flickered over Seth. She smiled sadly. "I thought I'd found a man with passion in his eyes, and I discovered how quickly passion dies when the money runs short. The ink had barely dried on my wedding certificate when my ex-husband discovered that my annuities couldn't support him in the manner to which he wanted to become accustomed."

"So you came back to Charleston," Seth concluded.

"Actually, no, not by choice."

Seth waited silently while Gloria sipped her tea to maintain her composure. He had the distinct feeling that Gloria hadn't revealed the final coup de grace to anyone.

"Carlos felt as though I'd cheated him. If you can't have the golden egg, the next best thing is to go where the hen roosts." Her humor had a double-edged blade that she aimed directly at herself. "He strung me along, long enough to get back to the land of golden opportunity and file for citizenship papers. When he felt safe, he flew the coop.''

Muttering a vile expletive, Seth commiserated with her.

"Ah, but poetic justice prevailed. Carlos remarried for the same reasons. You've heard the saying, 'Marry for money and spend the rest of your life earning it?' From what I've heard, his new wife's father put him to work as a laborer in one of their steel factories. Now that's hell, isn't it?''

Seth understood that kind of hell. He'd been a second-class citizen all his life. "Yeah," he agreed, empathizing without sympathy.

"And I have Pete. I nearly squandered the best thing in my life searching for adventure." She pointed to her eyes. "See? The hungry look vanished." Her finger turned toward Seth. "Yours is still there."

"Our situation isn't the same," he reminded her. "I left Charleston not by choice, but by necessity. I guess if there's any poetic justice in my case, it's my success. Everybody thought a young car thief would grow up to be a hardened criminal.''

"Vanessa and I often wondered what happened. You wouldn't care to enlighten me, would you?''

Seth's eyes narrowed speculatively as he weighed the pros and cons. He knew by telling Gloria, the truth would get back to Vanessa. It wouldn't clear his name, but at least she'd know he'd been a damned fool rather than a thief. But what difference would it make? He couldn't expect Vanessa to forsake Lee, scum though he was, and rush into his arms just because her grandfather had used his influence to separate them.

"No." To soften his negative reply, he added, "But thanks for asking. It's too late for the truth."

"Like hell," Gloria scoffed. "Vanessa needs to know the truth—all of it."

The vehemence in her voice alerted Seth to the possibility that he wasn't the only friend Vanessa had who knew about Lee's unfaithfulness. "You know, don't you?"

"That Lee Hayden is a first-class heel? The whole damned town knows, with the exceptions being the Haydens and the Monarchs."

"Dammit, Gloria, you're her friend. You're the last person who should stand by and let her be hurt. Why haven't you told her?"

"Vanessa is my only female friend. Uh-uh! Nobody likes the person who stands around with a pin in their hand, bursting bubbles. The Romans killed the bearers of bad tidings." She lowered her voice and whispered guiltily, "I know I'm being selfish. I should have told her last year, but I can't. She'd hate me. That's why—"

"You're here," Seth finished. "You want me to be the bad guy. You want me to deliver the bad news and then vamoose out of town. Thanks one helluva lot, Gloria."

When a lone tear brimmed from Gloria's eye and trickled down her face, leaving a trail of mascara, Seth was instantly contrite. Heaping recriminations on Gloria wasn't going to save Vanessa. Maybe if they pooled their resources they could come up with a viable solution.

"I'm sorry. Don't cry," Seth grumbled. Like most men, he didn't know how to deal with a woman's tears.

Wiping her eye with the corner of her linen napkin, Gloria sniffled. "I feel so rotten."

"Yeah. Me, too. I was awake half the night trying to figure out a way to tell her without having her hating me worse than she'll hate Lee."

"We shouldn't have to suffer for what someone else did," Gloria concurred.

Seth had been in that situation before now, but then he'd been young and inexperienced. Being caught in circumstances beyond his control hadn't sweetened with the passage of time.

"We could set him up," Gloria conspired. "Follow Lee when Charlotte is with him, then take Vanessa over there."

"Humiliate her in public? That'll endear us to Vanessa," Seth responded sarcastically. "That's worse than the idea I came up with—wrapping my hands around Lee's scrawny neck and choking a confession out of him."

Gloria leaned forward on her folded arms, whispering, "There is one weak link in the chain of silence surrounding Lee's secret affair."

"Are you thinking of who I think you're thinking?" Seth asked, shifting his position in the chair until their heads were almost touching.

"Who is the one person who would have something to gain?"

Vanessa checked her watch for the fiftieth time. She'd been waiting outside Gabriel's for over an hour.

A chilly wind blew between the open market stalls and the renovated storefronts. Mentally she kicked herself for not getting back into her car after the first five minutes had passed. Lee prided himself on being prompt.

She strode to the end of the block and glanced down the street toward the bank. "No fire trucks. No ambulances. No hurricane warnings," she muttered, thinking of the only acceptable excuses Lee would have for standing her up—fire, death or natural disaster.

As each minute had ticked by, she'd considered her alternatives. Standing on the street corner impatiently tapping her toe wasn't going to get her message across to Lee.

Dignity kept her from marching into the bank and confronting him. Her decision to postpone the wedding would cause enough of a scandal without the additional impropriety of informing Lee at his place of business. She wanted to be on neutral territory when she dropped her bomb.

Clenching her teeth in frustration, she started toward the Market Street parking lot where she'd left her car. She wondered if Lee had deliberately broken their appointment. He'd said that as far as he was concerned there was nothing to discuss. Did he think turning a deaf ear would silence her? Lee wasn't obtuse. He had to know from their previous conversation that the odds for them getting married Saturday were getting slimmer by the minute. Prewedding jitters weren't cured by breaking a luncheon date.

A hundred yards from her car the heavens opened, and rain poured from the sky like water out of a boot.

Within seconds Vanessa was drenched from head to toe.

Inside her LeBaron, Vanessa shivered, searching in her purse for the key to the car's ignition. She sneezed three times in quick succession. *A summer cold will round out my day perfectly,* she silently derided.

She found her key and started the engine. As she drove toward home to change clothes, she decided what she'd do. Lee had left her two choices. She could go through with the wedding as planned, or she could take drastic measures to get his attention.

"A two-by-four up the side of his head," she muttered, hitting the defroster button with one finger. She didn't care if she had to wait on his steps until dawn, once she'd changed clothes, she was going to camp there until she got her message across loud and clear.

Her spirits were gloomier than the clouds overhead by the time she had parked her car and made a mad dash through the courtyard.

"You should have taken an umbrella," she heard, louder than the raindrops, softer than the thudding of her feet running across the veranda.

"I should have stayed here and helped with lunch instead of standing on a street corner getting drenched," Vanessa huffed. She knew she looked like a soggy cream puff. Her ruffled white blouse had wilted, and the pleats of her navy blue skirt drooped unevenly. Seth appeared not to notice her bedraggled appearance. His eyes studied her, searching for what was beneath the surface.

"Your fiancé made a luncheon date and stood you up?" The thought of Vanessa standing in the rain while Lee was probably wining and dining Charlotte angered Seth. *So help me,* he silently fumed, *if she so much as sneezes, Lee's face is going to look as though it's gone through a meat grinder when I get finished with him!*

Vanessa saw the light flare in his eyes as he questioned her. She didn't want him fighting her battles. She fully intended to take Lee to task for his inconsideration.

"Yes, but I'll be seeing him tonight." *Whether Lee wants to see me or not,* she silently added.

Seth removed his handkerchief from his back pocket. "C'mere. I'll dry your face."

Tilting her face upward, Vanessa closed her eyes as he gently blotted droplets of water. "Remember how you bandaged my skinned knees when I fell down on the seawall?" she asked as his fingers began to work his special magic on her.

He remembered. She'd been imitating him, showing off. She'd teetered between falling on the rocks lining the seawall and falling on the sidewalk. He'd pushed her to the sidewalk.

"You were mad as a fly stuck on flypaper," he recalled. "You haughtily informed me that you were pretending to lose your balance. It was my fault you'd skinned your knees."

Vanessa grinned. "I was scared, but I wasn't about to admit that I'd come within inches of splitting my head open."

She was within inches of splitting her heart open now, Seth mused, wondering again if he should tell her about Lee. He wanted to protect her. He didn't want her hurt. And yet he knew if he figuratively pushed her for her own safety that she'd be mad as hell. He couldn't do it this time. She'd never forgive him.

Vanessa felt her heart racing faster and faster with each lingering swipe of his handkerchief. Silent arguments she'd suppressed warred in her mind.

I'm engaged. Then why is your heart pounding when you're near Seth?

Lee is an honorable man. So tell him how Seth makes you feel.

I don't want to hurt Lee. You'll be hurting him more by living a lie.

But I should love Lee. But do you?

Like a brother or a dear friend. So who wants to marry Beaver Cleaver when a living, breathing Rhett Butler is toe-to-toe with you?

I've got to postpone the wedding. Right!

I've got to avoid Seth until I've talked to Lee. Wrong! Seth isn't going to let you avoid him; you don't want to avoid him, either!

"Who's winning?" Seth murmured, amused by her facial expressions changing from a sappy grin to a stern scowl.

Their eyes met, skittered away, then were drawn back to each other.

Do I love Seth? she asked herself. Then she knew, without a doubt he was the reason she didn't want to marry Lee.

The question she'd avoided asking herself and the ensuing unwelcome answer rocked her back on her heels.

"Vanessa?" Seth said, speculating on what had caused her jaw to drop, her chin to wobble and the sharp shake of her head.

"I've got to go."

"Where? Why are you running from me?"

It was on the tip of her tongue to staunchly deny that she'd ever run from him. Running meant fear. There was no logical reason for her to fear Seth.

"Vanessa, tell me what I saw in your eyes is real." His forefinger thumped his chest. "Tell me what I'm feeling in here isn't wrong."

"I'm engaged!"

"Do you think I don't know that? Do you think that every time I get near you and want to kiss you that I forget you're going to marry another man on Saturday? Do you think I want to feel like my stomach is tied up in pretzel knots?" He held both of her arms to keep her from moving away from him. From the depths of his insecurities, he asked, "Do you think I came here to cause trouble for you?"

"No!"

"Then what am I supposed to do?"

Honest to God, Vanessa hadn't the foggiest notion of what they should do. She heard the heartache in his voice and wanted to soothe his pain as surely as she wanted to feel his lips on hers.

"I don't know," she mumbled. She struggled to verbalize how she felt. She jerked her arm free. "I feel...disloyal."

"You feel disloyal and I feel like hell," Seth muttered.

"Then we need to stay away from each other. It's a big house," she said, her arms waving. "I need to get my head on straight. I need to talk to Lee."

Letting Lee influence Vanessa was an abominable idea. He'd lied his way straight to the wedding altar. Lee wasn't going to level with Vanessa.

"You need to make your own decision."

She had, but she couldn't sneak around behind Lee's back. The least she owed Lee was to confront him, to tell him in plain English that she didn't love him, not the way a woman should love the man she'd planned to marry. In the meantime, she had no choice but to keep silent with Seth.

Seth knew he'd lost when he saw her mouth set in a stubborn line. He gazed at her helplessly as she started toward the door. Her slumped shoulders told him how hard the decision she'd made was for her.

"I don't suppose you could help out with the dinner crowd, could you?" she asked. She hated leaving him on such a sour note.

"I'd better not."

He turned toward the courtyard, unable to bear seeing her unhappy. He was in love with a woman who was engaged to another man, who was a rotten deceitful bastard.

While Seth silently flagellated himself for being ten kinds of a coward for not telling Vanessa exactly what kind of a skunk Lee was, Vanessa moved behind him.

"Seth, would you hold me? Just for a minute or two? That should be enough to get me through the night."

He couldn't deny her or himself a moment's physical respite from their mental anguish. Turning, he held his arms open to her.

"You feel so right," she whispered against his shirtfront.

Inane words that didn't express half of what he was feeling stumbled from Seth's mouth. "You feel good, too."

He closed his eyes and treasured the moment. Her hair felt soft and sleek as satin under his chin. His hands rubbed over the back of her damp blouse. She smelled of summer rain and sweet woman—a heady combination that left him a bit dizzy.

Vanessa matched the stroking of her hands on his back with what she felt along her spine. Her nose nuzzled into the freshness of his laundered shirt. Slightly withdrawing to look up at him, she felt Seth's hands cup her nape, tugging on a damp strand of hair.

"You'll have to forgive me for this kiss, too," he whispered, closing his mouth over hers. He'd been little more than a child when he'd first kissed her. He had paid a price for that kiss. As her lips parted beneath the pressure of his tongue, he knew this kiss was worth every lonely minute of his self-imposed exile. He kissed her with all the pent-up love he'd felt as a young man and now as an adult.

Vanessa met his tongue, tasting, savoring, etching his flavor on her memory. Her back pressed against the centuries-old pillar, supporting both of them as his hands molded her flesh to his as deftly as a master chef molding pastry into pie tins. She slanted her head, opening wider for him. One kiss became two, then three, then a multitude of tiny kisses peppered across her cheeks, chin and neck.

"There's nothing to forgive. I only wish you had come back sooner," Vanessa whispered as she arched her neck to give him free access to the sensitive places he'd missed on his first foray.

"I needed my father's invitation—an excuse." He showered her neck with dewy kisses, leaving her skin as damp as when she'd first stepped in from the rain.

Vanessa flicked the tip of his earlobe. "Charles missed you. We all missed you."

I love you, she silently declared. Later, after she did the honorable thing by talking to Lee first, she would tell him just how much she loved him. She would show him how much she had missed him.

Seth felt himself sliding far beyond the boundaries she'd set when she asked him to hold her. She'd kissed him with the hunger of a woman who wanted a man. Knowing she wanted him was worse than having doubts. How could he stop, knowing that this kiss could be their last kiss? He wanted to love her completely.

"We'd better stop," Vanessa said halfheartedly, wanting to go on and on and never look back.

Seth rocked his forehead against hers, vainly trying to break physical contact with her because she'd told him to stop, but not quite being able to release her.

It was Vanessa who took the first hesitant step sideways, out of his arms. Her eyes lowered to her fingers, which remained on his shirtfront. Later, her eyes promised soulfully. Later. She would come to Seth with the same dignity and pride in herself that he'd had when he'd arrived from New York.

Five

——

THE WEDDING IS OFF.

Vanessa slipped the note she'd penned under Lee's front door. A grandfather clock in a nearby apartment struck its twelfth gong.

Midnight, and all is well, Vanessa mused. Alleviated from the state of indecision that had worried her, she felt ten years younger and a hundred pounds lighter.

Her steps were buoyant as she started down the thickly carpeted flights of stairs to the main floor entry hall. She felt like a butterfly whose wings had been pinned to a display board, then had unexpectedly been set free. Lighthearted, she had to resist the impulse to ride the banister to the bottom floor.

Halfway down the first flight, she heard the front door slam. Loud voices carried up the steps.

"You can't marry her," an unrecognizable feminine voice implored. "Lee, for heaven's sake, I'm carrying your child!"

"Keep your voice down. Do you want the entire building to know you're a liar? You said you were on the Pill. What possessed you to think I'd change my plans just because you decided to get pregnant? Dammit, you knew I planned on marrying Vanessa. You said you didn't care... that you loved me."

Stunned, Vanessa grabbed the banister when she heard Lee's name spoken. Lee? Her Lee? With another woman? It couldn't be Lee Hayden. She looked down, but was unable to see the man, or the woman with him. Her head spun dizzily as she heard his callous reply. Her fiancé was going to be the father of another woman's child? She heard Lee's heavy footstep hit the first stair.

Completely knocked for a loop, she staggered backward. Her rubbery legs threatened to buckle. She had to get out of there before they discovered her. Vanessa retreated farther up the staircase to the next landing.

"I do love you," the woman whispered, her voice spiraling up the staircase. "I know you didn't promise me anything, but I thought—"

"You're damn right I didn't make false promises."

"You made love to me. Your body shouts that fact each time we make love. I know you love me!" she wailed. "Lee, you can't marry her! Please, please, I can't believe you'd marry someone else."

"Come to the Methodist church Saturday and watch me."

A cold shiver went up Vanessa's spine as she heard scuffling on the landing below her. Listening carefully, she heard a low guttural moan, but it wasn't one of pain or agony. She peeked over the rail. Lee was kissing the woman she'd seen at the bank! Charlotte something-or-another!

He'd never kissed Vanessa that way.

Seth had.

She remembered feeling Seth's hard body holding her as though his life depended on her.

Charlotte circled her arms around Lee's neck, devouring his lips in desperation.

Vanessa averted her eyes. What she had seen was too special, too intimate for a third party to witness. Each kiss Lee peppered along Charlotte's throat had the effect of a blowtorch scorching Vanessa's pride until it was reduced to ashes.

Lee Hayden was a complete stranger to her.

She'd known Lee all her life, been his girl, worn his college ring, and yet the man caressing the woman downstairs was a total stranger. A despicable stranger, she amended.

Lee had presented his best side to her, but it had been an illusion. She'd credited him as being a man with high moral standards. Honorable. Lee Hayden had no honor, no integrity, or he would have broken up with her months ago, years ago.

Her stomach churned when she heard Charlotte whispering, "Yes. Love me, Lee."

Fool, Vanessa wanted to shout. Trapped on the floor above the lovers, she wanted to bellow, *Why, Lee? Why did you ask me to marry you?* But she couldn't. She had to sit there, huddled with her arms about her knees, and keep the rage bottled inside of her.

Moments later, she heard the door to Lee's apartment open. She peeked between the rails and saw Lee sweep his lover into his arms. He kicked the door closed with his foot. Eager to get Charlotte into his bedroom, he'd been too anxious to turn on the light.

Before he closed the door, Vanessa saw the paper she'd slipped under his door earlier. It was beneath the sole of Lee's shoe. The ball of his foot ground the slip of paper into the carpet just as Lee had ground her pride into the dirt.

Vanessa slowly rose, her cramped legs creaking in protest. She hadn't aged during those few minutes, but she'd had her eyes opened up. Stoically she moved down the steps, swiftly, silently.

Outside, she touched the area over her heart. It should hurt, she thought. She felt nothing. No thudding. No pounding blood. No pain. Nothing.

Lee's treachery should have left her feeling heartsick. But most of her bitterness was directed at the mental cruelty Lee was inflicting on Charlotte. While he was kissing her, he was tearing Charlotte's self-esteem to shreds.

Considering what she'd just seen and heard, the guilt she'd felt when she'd written Lee the note paled in significance. He'd hoodwinked her into believing he respected her. Respect? she silently spat. Lee didn't comprehend the meaning of the word.

"I have to work late," she muttered, recalling the puny excuse he'd given her, one she'd believed. Lord have mercy, he must have been snickering up his sleeve when she'd encouraged him to give Charlotte what she wanted. Charlotte had come to the bank wanting him, and she had got him, at least in a physical sense.

Lee had treated them both badly.

He'd promised Vanessa love, passion and devotion. He'd given them to another woman to whom he'd refused to make any promises. Which was the cruelest? She honestly didn't know.

His false promises stung Vanessa's pride, but it was a small, insignificant sting compared to what could have happened if she'd married him. Months, maybe years, down the road, she would eventually have discovered his duplicity. It would have destroyed her pride to know that her husband had a mistress...a baby by another woman. By then, they might have had children of their own. Regardless, she knew she would have had the inner strength to cut Lee out of her life.

As she strode to the car, she remembered wishing Charlotte good luck. How had she replied? "Sometimes we have to make our own luck." Vanessa had heard luck came in two flavors—good and bad. She could taste the flavor of good luck on her tongue.

She'd been lucky, she decided as she entered her car and drove back home. Better to have found out before the wedding than afterward.

Clearheaded, she arrived at The Butterfly with a list of things she had to accomplish. The task she dreaded the most was at the top of her list. Her grandfather had to be informed of the change of plans. After talking to the Colonel, informing the minister would be simple. Gloria, her maid of honor, would be the most understanding since she'd never been overly fond of Lee.

The wedding gifts she'd received had to be returned. She didn't want anything with Lee's name on it stored in her home. She'd take the guest list she'd used to write out the wedding invitations and drop each guest a personal note.

She hadn't the vaguest idea what she'd write. The truth? she mused, wondering if there would be a run on the Hayden Bank if the good citizens of Charleston realized what an underhanded sneak was handling their money.

No, she decided. She wasn't interested in getting even with Lee. Revenge was for people who'd been hurt, who'd suffered. She'd been deceived, but knowing Lee loved another woman didn't hurt. She wouldn't stoop to his level by using a poison pen when she wrote the notes.

She parked her car outside the two-story carriage house. Seth and Charles would be upstairs in Charles's apartment. She didn't want to awaken them.

Glancing upward, she included Seth's name on the list of people she had to inform of the changes in her plans. She wondered how he'd react. Her eyes dropped to the place on her arms where he'd held her, demanding to know if Lee had mistreated her. Seth would pound the starch right out of Lee's white shirt, she silently mused, frowning. And she knew precisely how Lee would react. Lee would call the police and have Seth arrested for assault and battery. She didn't want Seth in trouble, not for her sake. Loathing the scenario she imagined, she decided she'd better delete any reference to what she'd seen and heard when she told Seth she'd cancelled the weddding.

She'd tell Seth it wasn't Gloria and Pete she'd been worried about; it was Lee and herself. Since he'd been unable to comprehend the lack of sexual attraction between herself and Lee, she'd tell him she'd backed out of the wedding because Lee didn't physically appeal to her.

That wasn't a lie. Knowing what she now knew, making love with Lee was physically repulsive!

Silently she crossed the courtyard toward the side entrance of the main house. Tomorrow would be the first day of a new life, she decided. A life without Lee Hayden playing a major role.

"Vanessa..."

A whisper from above her weaved its way through the long, dangling blooms of wisteria, through the length of Spanish moss clinging to the century-old live oaks.

In the darkness she looked upward, but couldn't see anyone.

"Vanessa... wait."

Shivers tingled up her spine. As a child, she'd created a Civil War fairy tale of a maiden who'd sit in the courtyard waiting for her dashing cavalry officer to appear from nowhere and save the Monarch plantation house.

The rhythmic sound of muffled steps coming down the stairs of the carriage house reminded Vanessa of muffled horse's hooves in a distance.

Seeing Seth move toward her, she had to mentally shake herself out of the fantasy. He wasn't her Confederate hero dressed in gray with elaborate gold braid. Bare chested, barefooted, the snap of his jeans open,

Seth's lack of clothing was far more devastating to her senses than the hero of her fantasy.

"What are you doing up?" she asked softly so as not to disturb Seth's father or her grandfather.

"Waiting to make certain you got home safely. I was worried that something might have happened to you."

Moonlight filtering through the branches overhead distorted the reddish tints in Vanessa's hair, turning them to silver streaks. He stopped within inches of her, hooking his thumbs into the empty belt loops of his jeans to keep from raking the silky sweep of hair away from her face.

Something has happened, she wanted to say. *In less than five minutes the whole course of my life was changed. Nothing is the way I thought it was.*

Lee was completely out of her life.

There was nothing morally or ethically that could stop her from kissing Seth.

It could have been her damaged pride that needed to be soothed by Seth's desire. It could have been the unrequited passion she'd housed in her body. It could have been a kiss that had been interrupted years ago that made Vanessa reach for Seth. She didn't know or care. Tomorrow, when she was sane and rational, she would blame it on the man in the moon if something or someone was to blame for closing the gap between Seth and herself.

Mutely she placed the palms of her hands on Seth's bare chest. This afternoon she'd felt the fine texture of his shirt. Now she splayed her fingers and tactilely gorged on the texture of his warm skin. She heard his sharp intake of breath. Her forefinger and thumb boldly traced the hardened nub of his nipple. Without his touching her, her breasts felt heavy, yearning to feel hands over them.

Seth mustered control from his rapidly depleting reserves. A small muscle on his jaw rebelled, twitching as the crown of Vanessa's hair brushed against it.

"What happened?" His voice sounded hoarse, but he couldn't control his vocal cords any better than he controlled the pounding of his heart.

What happened before she touched Seth was unimportant to Vanessa. "Nothing important," she whispered truthfully, brushing her lips along the path her fingers explored. He smelled of soap—clean and inviting. She inhaled, taking his fragrance deep inside her. "What's going to happen is what's important."

"Vanessa..." He soughed a feeble protest. How could he possibly stop what he ardently wanted? As a teenager, how often had he sprawled across his bed, stared down at the courtyard and dreamed of Vanessa calling his name, beckoning him to come lie with her? How painfully he had yearned for her.

She'd been too young to know what power she held over him. She had been his champion, his tormentor, his secret love. If making love with her was a crime, he was a willing accomplice. He'd serve twenty years in the military for one night with her.

Vanessa's fingertips lingered in the sensitive hollow formed by his collarbone, then trekked upward until her thumbs followed the natural curve of his bottom lip. His lips trembled, parting, letting her feel his life's breath.

Seth sensed her need to provocatively arouse him. He sensed that she wanted more than slow, reassuring caresses. She wanted more than softness and sweetness. She wanted to know he desired her, that he wanted her.

His hands moved to rest on her hips, letting her physically feel the proof of her success. He murmured a meaningless sound of pleasure. He knew she was innocent, and yet he knew he wouldn't hurt her.

"Kiss me, Vanessa," he huskily encouraged her. Uttering a low groan filled with savage need, he covered her mouth with his, gently rocking their lips together and swaying her hips against him. He felt her body stir, awakening, blazing into life.

Seth wanted sweet, fragile Vanessa Monarch with every fiber of his being. He slanted his mouth from one side to the other until he'd kissed her senseless. Haste had marred their first kiss; frustration and disloyalty had tainted their second kiss; he wouldn't let that happen tonight.

Long-submerged feminine instincts exploded in a spray of fireworks behind Vanessa's eyelids. Seth's teeth nipped an erotic path along her bottom lip until her hands clasped behind his head, demanding him to stop the teasing forays his tongue made.

She wanted him inside her. She wanted to fully taste his passion. Seth obliged with one quick thrust of his tongue.

Vanessa moaned, the small sound lost in his mouth as he deepened the kiss. *Love me,* her heart silently cried. Perhaps later, when she was sane, she'd realize Lee had hurt more than just her pride. With each flaming kiss she'd witnessed between Lee and Charlotte, her subconscious had been sorely wounded. Lee had made her feel less of a woman; ugly, unwanted and undesirable.

Seth's passion soothed those angry, raw wounds. Held tightly in his strong arms, his tongue twining with hers, she felt beautiful, desirable, wanted.

The sensation of being slowly lowered to the dewy grass was lost on Vanessa. She only felt herself climbing higher and higher toward the shimmering promise of fulfillment.

Fog, nature's blanket of privacy, cloaked the courtyard, ensuring their privacy from prying eyes.

"Vanessa, you've always made my blood run hot," Seth whispered, tormenting the lobe of her ear with his tongue. Nimbly his fingers undid the front of her blouse. "In my mind I've made love with you hundreds of times. I've lain awake and thought about your hair, your lips, your breasts." His fingers parted her blouse, trailing over the feminine curve beneath her lacy bra. Her nipples stiffened in response to his light caress. "You're so beautiful. Let me make love to you, sweet Vanessa. Be my woman." *If only for tonight,* he silently completed, knowing he could be damning himself to an eternity of knowing she'd never be his again.

"Yes," she assented, "love me, Seth. Make me yours."

Slowly his hand smoothed down the length of her body.

Seth longed to tell her he loved her, but he didn't dare. He'd bargained for one night, one night of believing she was completely his. He wouldn't burden her with his love. What he couldn't say he expressed in the fervent kisses he pressed on her lips, her cheeks, her throat.

Vanessa longed to tell him what had happened earlier. She was free of her entanglement with Lee. Without any emotional reservations she would be Seth's woman. The urgency of his kisses swept her beyond reason. Her senses spun crazily as his hand skimmed from her breasts, over the flat contour of her stomach, along her upper thigh. Goose bumps raised when his hand stroked her bare calf beneath her skirt, then with agonizing slowness, climbed higher and higher. She caught her breath.

Seth heard her gasp and silently cursed himself for rushing her. "Don't be shy with me," he crooned softly. Light as a butterfly's wings, his hand flew over her silken thigh. "I'd never hurt you."

Vanessa reached down and covered his hand with hers. She couldn't stop the trembling he'd caused, but it wasn't because she was physically afraid of him. She had to tell him it wasn't Gloria she'd been talking about the other day. How was she going to tell him she'd reached the ripe old age of twenty-six, been engaged and never experienced such sweet torment? She swallowed hard, attempting to gather her wits long enough to explain.

"I know you haven't let another man touch you like this."

Surprised and somewhat flustered that he'd readily seen through her white lie, she blurted, "You do?"

"Lee must be dead from the neck down. How he could have been engaged to you and done nothing more than hold your hand is beyond me. All I have to do is look at you and my body turns hard as an oak tree.''

"I like having you touch me," she said, running her hand over his naked chest. She felt his stomach muscles quiver beneath her hand. She gloried in the fact that he trembled at her lightest caress. "I like touching you. You weren't the only one who was lying awake at night. After you left, I used to touch my lips and wonder what could have happened that night."

"God, Vanessa. You were so young. I must have been temporarily insane to go to you." His fingers shook as he unhooked the front clip of her bra, gingerly parting the lacy cups. He palmed the fullness of her breast. His thumb circled the tip until it was rigid. His eyes widened hungrily. Her breasts were beautiful, perfect, more than he'd ever dreamed. "These used to drive me crazy."

Gentle hands, Vanessa thought when he lazily rotated his thumb over one peak, then the other. Utter recklessness coursed through her. Her hands kneaded his chest as his lips, tongue and teeth tasted her. The achy feeling of full arousal drew her knees upward, parting them.

I love you, she thought silently. *Oh, Seth, I've loved you forever.*

Her hands moved to his back when he lowered his bare flesh to hers. Was it his moan of pleasure that whispered over the blades of dewy grass, or hers? she wondered. She shifted her shoulders slightly from side to side to get the maximum amount of contact with him as he removed the cloth barrier he'd previously pushed aside.

There's no stopping, Seth thought, his mind a tangled web of taste, smell and touch. He showered tiny kisses over her as his thumbs hooked beneath the elastic waistbands of her skirt, slip and panties. In one agile swoop, he dispensed with her clothing.

And then he stopped.

She's too perfect for you, he silently demeaned. She'll regret this come dawn. What happens if she arrives in church on Saturday with your baby growing inside of her? Dammit, man, you can wreck your life, but don't louse up hers.

Vanessa felt him straighten his elbows until they were locked. Her fingers caught the tab of his zipper between them and tugged none too gently.

"Help me," she coaxed. His one arm blocked her from using both hands. "Please."

"You don't know what you're asking," Seth said, his jaw clenched so tightly that his lips barely moved. *Give me the strength,* he prayed, *to get up, get her dressed and take her to the safety of her room.*

Her inexperience was damned embarrassing to her, but her determination grew. She'd get that zipper down if she had to do it with her teeth. That proved unnecessary as it suddenly gave. Her arm twined around his waist, inching his jeans lower, sensuously rubbing against his backside with her forearm as her breasts swayed against his front.

Seth's control along with his good intentions to stop were blasted to smithereens when he felt himself intimately pressed against Vanessa. He rolled over her and kicked off his jeans.

Vanessa felt his hands everywhere at once. His mouth moved against her body. His teeth nipped at places he'd longed to touch. Her hands dove into his dark hair as her back arched against his hips.

"Love me," she begged. "Now."

She isn't ready, he thought, striving to keep control over his desire to swiftly plunge deeply inside her. He touched her intimately; she was afire. Her hips twisted beneath his hand, demanding satisfaction.

Seth took a deep breath, then covered her mouth with his as he entered her. His tongue sent love messages to her, telling her not to be afraid, that he'd make their loving as painless as he possibly could.

Vanessa was deaf to his silent communication. She was sexually a late bloomer, but the passion she'd contained had finally been released. She didn't want to be treated like a porcelain figure on a pedestal any longer. Her long legs wrapped around him, pulling him deeply inside her. Her eyes opened as he penetrated the thin virginal barrier, but there was no pain, only the jubilant knowledge that she was Seth Kimble's lover.

Her eyes filled with tears of joy.

"Did I hurt you?" Seth asked, trying not to move, trying to remain perfectly still until she adjusted to him.

"No. Don't stop. Please, don't stop. I feel . . ." She didn't know what she felt or how to say it. Somehow she felt suspended between heaven and hell. There was more to making love. She knew that. But it wasn't until she felt him moving inside her that she knew he would be taking her to the highest pinnacle of pleasure. Her body rocked against him, adjusting to his rhythm. She could hardly believe the level of pleasure could rise, but it did. It grew and mounted until it possessed her. "Oh, yes, Seth, yes."

She clung to him, loving him, wildly urging him on to the oneness that she knew was the place in heaven that he'd specially reserved for her. Her dreams of loving him were nondescript black-and-white compared to the vivid colors splashing behind her eyelids. The yellows of yearning and reds of passion and finally, the greens of peaceful fulfillment splattered in glorious Technicolor.

Later, when their ragged breathing had subsided, she heard Seth whispering to her. She heard him say that he'd take her inside, but her body was too limp to respond. She was beyond caring where they were as long as they were together. Through lowered lashes she watched him put on his jeans and gather her clothing.

She appreciated the strength in his arms when he stooped and lifted her high against his chest. Sighing, Vanessa felt light as a cloud.

Seth carried her up the side steps. Fleetingly he wondered what he'd say if her grandfather appeared, but he quickly decided the Fates had been kind this time. Instead he worried about Vanessa's silence. Was she already regretting what had taken place between them? Was she wondering what she'd tell Lee on their wedding night?

Seth had a few things he planned on telling Lee. None of them were nice. Three days, he silently groaned. Three days in which to refine the plan he and Gloria had hatched up between them. Once Vanessa knew what a rat Lee Hayden was, then maybe, just maybe, she'd consider marrying Seth. She wouldn't be able to forget his past, but maybe he could convince her that he did have a solid future, one he wanted to share with her.

After he'd tucked Vanessa safely into her bed and given her a long, lingering kiss, he went back to the carriage house apartment. Although he was physically satiated, his mind was cluttered with old doubts and fears. His fist pounding the pillow didn't soften the facts: Vanessa Monarch was too far above him socially, morally and mentally. She wouldn't marry him—not in a million years.

Gloria bounced on the end of the canopy bed, jarring Vanessa awake. "Rise and shine, little Monarch butterfly. It's a beautiful morning in Charleston and you're going to miss it."

"I'll take a rain check," Vanessa muttered, curling into a tight ball and pulling the coverlet over her head. Her dreams had been so sweet, so wonderful, that she was reluctant to face daylight.

The coverlet jerked from her hands. A spray of water splattered on her face.

"I told you she'd need the water treatment," Seth said, wiping the remainder of water from his fingertips onto his jeans. When Gloria had arrived at his doorstep to institute phase one of their master plan, he'd decided to act as though nothing had changed between Vanessa and himself. He honestly didn't know if Vanessa would confide in Gloria, but he didn't want to take the chance of compromising the woman he loved. "Come on, Vanessa. We've got a big day planned for you."

Being spritzed by water and knowing Seth was in her room dissipated the last vestiges of her fabulous dream. It wasn't a dream, she thought, tenderly moving her hand beneath the cover until she touched a tender spot where his whiskers had lightly abraded her skin. Opening one eye, she saw the devilish grin on Seth's face and wanted to pelt him. Having water dribbled on her wasn't her idea of pillow talk.

Vanessa saw Seth wink and nod in Gloria's direction. She understood completely. He wanted to keep what they'd shared as their own private secret. Inwardly smiling, Vanessa scolded, "Seth Kimble, you know I'm going to get your big toe for giving me the water treatment."

Chuckling, Seth explained to Gloria, "The big toe on my right foot is three inches longer than the one on my left foot, from Vanessa being the first one to wake up. She's merciless."

"Oh, go bake a cake," Vanessa blurted before thinking.

"Cake is baked." Nudging Gloria in the ribs he added, "Gloria is going to help put the icing on the cake. Right, Gloria?"

Vanessa knew the two of them were up to something when she heard the wicked giggle bubbling from Gloria's mouth.

Straightening her legs, she grabbed the sheet, held it against her chest and rolled to an upright position. "Gloria, you aren't in cahoots with him, are you?"

"Say no," Seth coaxed from the side of his mouth. "Otherwise, you'll have to buy two pairs of satin bridesmaid's slippers to wear to her wedding."

Gloria gave Vanessa her best wide-eyed, innocent look. "Me?"

Seth's mention of her wedding served as a total eye-opener for Vanessa. After last night, how could he joke about her marrying another man? She hadn't come right out and told him she wasn't marrying Lee, but surely he knew.

"I called off the wedding," Vanessa blurted baldly.

"Now she's pulling my leg instead of my toe," Seth muttered dryly to Gloria. Who did she think she was kidding? Herself or him? Last night the first thing she would have told him before they made love was that she'd given Lee Hayden his walking papers.

"I don't think so." Gloria scrambled up the length of the bed and pushed Vanessa back against the pillows. "You are serious, aren't you?"

"Yeah." Vanessa's eyes ricocheted from Gloria's spreading grin to Seth's face. His eyes blazed with an inner light, and a smile that rivaled the sun for brightness lit the room.

Seth felt a hot surge of desire for Vanessa. The lady had to have guts to call off the wedding during the final countdown of days. For a fraction of a second he wondered what had caused the final break.

"Looks like we won't have to put plan A into effect," Gloria crowed, grinning up at Seth.

Vanessa saw the sharp glance Seth shot Gloria. "Plan A?"

"Attack and annihilate," Gloria agilely alliterated. "If necessary, assassinate."

Seth breathed more easily. For a moment he had feared Gloria would blab the real plan they'd hatched up the previous afternoon. The Dirty Half-A-Dozen was what Gloria had dubbed her plan to get Lee and Vanessa, Seth and Charlotte, and Pete and herself together for an evening of uncivilized warfare. The Butterfly was to be the war zone, with the Colonel present to witness the destruction.

"Charming," Vanessa commented drolly. No telling what they'd have done if they'd seen Lee passionately embracing Charlotte last night, she silently mused. Nothing nonviolent, she felt certain.

Gloria warmed up to the idea of completely throwing Vanessa off track from what they'd actually planned on doing. "Plan B was Seth's favorite. Black eye, broken nose, busted bones." On a roll, Gloria continued outrageously, "I voted for Plan C...castrate without cauterization!"

"I'd hate to hear what you two would plan to do to someone you really hated," Vanessa said, certain Gloria would go from A to Z unless stopped. "It's a wonder Carlos survived."

"Carlos wasn't worth the energy," Gloria quipped, satisfied that her dearest friend knew what drastic measures they would have taken to keep her from marrying Lee.

"Why did you call off the wedding?" Seth asked, needing to know if Vanessa had discovered the truth about Lee. Plans A, B and C combined were too good for Lee if she had.

Vanessa motioned for Gloria to hand her the robe hanging on the door of her closet. "Lack of interest," she lied glibly. Avoiding his penetrating gaze that could detect the slightest prevarication on her part, Vanessa's eyes followed Gloria as she bounced off the bed. Gloria tossed her the robe, and Vanessa pretended to concentrate on pushing her arms into the sleeves. To distract him further from Lee's infidelity, she added, "Before you and Gloria started hatching up plans, she must have told you that the tête-à-tête you and I had yesterday was actually about Lee and myself."

Plausible, Seth mused, watching her hand flit from straightening the collar of her robe to the sash. But inconceivable, he decided, fairly certain Lee wouldn't have tolerated a change in plans without making a commotion. From what he'd seen and heard, Lee was the sort of man who planned on having his cake and eating it, too. Lee wouldn't take kindly to having his cake, Vanessa, removed from his diet.

"How did Lee take the news?" Gloria asked. "Is he upset?"

Gloria's curiosity saved Seth from asking the same question.

Remembering how Lee had stepped on her note, Vanessa replied truthfully, "He wasn't upset." The strange look both of them gave her served as a silent warning that any man who'd been jilted three days before the big event wouldn't take it gracefully. "I think his mind was preoccupied—the state's bank examiners are rumored to be on their way to Charleston to audit his dad's bank."

"Did you postpone the wedding or call it off?" Seth asked in an effort to read between the lines of what she was saying and what she actually meant. Something wasn't right. For some unknown reason, Vanessa was protecting Lee. Why? he wondered. Did she still love the rotten SOB?

"It's definitely off." Vanessa looked Seth straight in the eye as she firmly answered his question. "I'm not marrying Lee Hayden this Saturday or any other day."

Pounding on the downstairs door stalled Seth from ferreting out the whole truth.

"Seth, would you mind getting that?" Vanessa asked.

"Somebody in the kitchen can answer it. Tell us exactly what Lee said."

"It's Wednesday. The Butterfly is closed on Wednesdays, remember?" Gloria moved toward the bedroom door as the knocking increased in volume. Before she could offer to answer it, Vanessa said, "Gloria, I'll need your help boxing up the wedding gifts to return them."

"Flowers," the three of them heard being bellowed from the veranda.

"Flowers?" Seth pinned Vanessa with his troubled eyes.

Vanessa had no ready explanation. The wedding flowers were to be delivered to the church Saturday morning. Flowers for the dining room had been delivered Monday. She hadn't the vaguest notion as to why flowers were being delivered. "The florist must have made a mistake."

Gloria was the first one through the door, quickly followed by Seth.

Vanessa flung the bedclothes aside and slipped her feet into her fuzzy house slippers. After what she'd witnessed with her own eyes the night before, Lee probably should have sent her buckets full of flowers, but flowers weren't going to change her mind. Quite by mistake, she'd been led to believe that Lee was a gentleman, but sending flowers to the woman who'd just jilted him exceeded courtly behavior. She absolutely would not consider the possibility that Lee hadn't read her note by this late in the morning. Either Lee or Charlotte must have seen it by now. Lee might choose to ignore what she'd written, but Charlotte wouldn't. The flowers couldn't be from Lee, she decided emphatically.

"Oh, my God!" Vanessa heard Gloria gasp. "I haven't seen that many roses since I went to the Rose Bowl football game! The whole porch is covered with vases of long-stemmed red roses."

"Vanessa!" Seth roared.

Shaking her fist in the direction of Lee's apartment, Vanessa called sweetly from the banister overhead, "There's been a mistake. Send them back, please."

"No way, lady," the delivery man shouted. "I'm to deliver the roses, then drive over to Mr. Hayden's place, show him my empty truck and collect my tip."

"Vanessa! I think you'd better get down here and read the card," Seth bellowed, holding a sealed envelope in his hand as though it were a time bomb set to explode momentarily.

Uncertain of whether she was coming or going, her mind in a complete tizzy, Vanessa went down the steps. Why was Lee sending flowers and making damned certain they were delivered? For a man who specialized in reading fine print, he should have been able to decipher what she'd written in big bold letters.

Nearing the bottom step, she could smell the fragrance of hundreds of roses coming through the open door. Gloria's eyes were the size of half-dollars. Seth looked fit to be tied. She couldn't falter, not now, not with Seth watching her every move.

"Just sign here, lady."

Her fingers were numb, ice-cold, barely able to curl around the pen being offered. She scrawled her name on the receipt as she heard the delivery man brag, "I picked up roses from every shop in town. You must be the luckiest lady in Charleston."

Vanessa swallowed and gave him a thin smile. The taste of bad luck coated her tongue. She wasn't going to be able to fib her way out of this one. How was she going to avoid telling Seth that she'd seen Lee with another woman? Without stopping long enough to consider the consequences, she knew Seth would carry out Plan B instantly—maybe Plan C.

While Vanessa took her own sweet time signing the receipt, Seth's stomach twisted into more knots than there were roses. His mouth hardened. He'd known there was something she'd been hiding. He waited until the delivery man had gone before he asked in an all-too-calm voice, "Aren't you going to read the card your fiancé sent? Out loud, please."

She heard the grim anger in his voice, slit the envelope, took a deep breath and removed the card. Quickly she scanned Lee's handwritten note: One rose for each apology I owe you for missing our luncheon date. I had to leave town unexpectedly. I'll be back Friday. Call when you've forgiven me. Deepest love, Lee.

Out of town? Forgive him? That lying snake in the grass. He'd freeze in hell before she considered forgiving him!

"Well?" Gloria asked, standing on tiptoe, trying to read over Vanessa's shoulder. "Is he broken-hearted—I hope."

Stalling, after vainly searching her brain for a king-size whopper to tell and failing, she replied, "Not exactly."

"The wedding is still on for Saturday," Seth conjectured. He should have known Vanessa calling off the wedding was too good to be true. They'd had a small disagreement, nothing that several dozen roses couldn't fix. Nothing that even making love with him in the darkness of the courtyard could change. The sickening sweet smell of Lee's form of apology gagged him.

Eyes lowered, Vanessa saw his hands clench and unclench. Choose the wrong answer and you'll have to watch him get thrown out of town by the police, she mentally cautioned. She couldn't let that happen.

Gloria breathed down the back of her neck and started to read, "One rose for each... Hey, don't stick it in your pocket."

"Gloria, thy name is cat," Vanessa warned, evading Seth's direct question. "You know what happens to curious cats, don't you?"

"I'm your best friend. Share!" Gloria protested as she attempted to reach into Vanessa's robe pocket.

"Okay." She wadded the note in her fist. "You take the roses. I'll keep the note."

"And I get the thorns," Seth muttered under his breath. "You don't have to explain, Vanessa. I get the picture. You'll have to excuse me. I have icing to make for the wedding cake."

Seth wheeled around and was out the door before Vanessa could stop him. For his sake, she couldn't tell the truth; for her sake, she couldn't lie.

"I'm not marrying Lee."

"That's a relief," Gloria gushed. "For a minute there, I was worried. Why'd Lee send the roses?"

"He didn't read my note."

"You wrote a note? You didn't tell him face-to-face?"

Gritting her teeth, Vanessa started back up the steps with Gloria hot on her heels. "I couldn't get close enough to his face to tell him. He broke our luncheon date. I waited for him at his condo until midnight...." Vanessa paused, winded by anger and frustration.

"Yes, go on," Gloria prompted.

"I wrote him a note, stuck it under his door and came home." Delete, delete, delete, Vanessa silently thought. Gloria and Seth being conspiratorial buddies eliminated Gloria as a confidante; Gloria would hightail it straight to the kitchen to tell Seth about Lee's duplicity. Sharing her problem would only complicate it.

"Maybe he ordered the roses yesterday," Gloria ventured.

"Or he hasn't found the note...." He'd found it. The roses, the note, the apology were all a hoax. Lee might think he'd outsmarted her by delaying the inevitable until Friday, but he had another think coming just as soon as she could get rid of Gloria, get dressed and go to his apartment.

"And thinks you're still going to get married." Gloria finished Vanessa's statement as though it were a death sentence.

Vanessa stopped on the landing, feeling as though she'd reached the top step of a gallows. Stopping a wedding at the last minute when the groom didn't want it stopped was proving more difficult than Gloria getting her divorce.

"You go and stop Seth from preparing the icing," Vanessa said, her mind considering several plans of action. "If Lee wants to play it cagey, I'll show him cagey. Before Saturday night is over, he'll wish he'd never tangled with a Monarch."

Six

Locating Charlotte was easy. Vanessa looked her name, number and address up in the Charleston telephone directory. She'd considered confronting Lee, but decided a private chat with Lee's girlfriend could be mutually beneficial. On her way to Charlotte's house, she mentally rehearsed what she'd say.

Basically, take-Lee-with-my-blessings was the main thrust of her thoughts.

Then she'd be free to fly away with Seth, she mused, grinning at her reflection in the rearview mirror. Just thinking of him brought a rosy glow to her pale cheeks. Last night he had brought every fantasy she'd had of him to life.

His lips had the tangy flavor of passion. Once tasted, Vanessa knew she couldn't settle for a flavorless, platonic love.

She was in love, really in love.

The kisses she'd shared with Lee were a watered-down version of what true love was all about. She still couldn't imagine why Lee wanted to marry her, but whatever reasons he had were unimportant. He didn't love her. Hell, he didn't even want her to share his bed.

Respect, Vanessa silently mused, partially accounted for Lee's determination to get her to the altar. Longevity in Charleston had given both the Monarch family and Hayden family influence. Everyone would view their marriage as two old families uniting, the perfect match.

"Someone should have informed Lee that marriages of convenience are a relic of the past."

Did Lee see her from the perspective of a collector of valuable antiques? Did he think he could put her in his home for his friends and business associates to come by and admire? He had made it plain as the aristocratic nose on his face that he preferred for her to be a housewife.

"And while I'm stuck on a shelf in his house, being the perfect wife, he's finding love elsewhere in Charlotte's arms."

Lee wanted Charlotte; Charlotte wanted Lee.

Lee was shortchanging Charlotte, too. He was giving her love and passion, but he was withholding respectability. Charlotte was good enough for Lee to use to slake his physical needs, and yet she wasn't good enough to share his name.

Until last night, Vanessa hadn't understood the meaning of the word snobbery. Lee had compartmentalized his life—acceptable and unacceptable, good women and bad women, love and passion. Vanessa filled one compartment and Charlotte filled the other.

Vanessa turned north on Smith Street and began searching for the right address. Row houses lined the street. They didn't compare to the lavish mansions in the Battery area, but they appeared neat and tidy. She located the correct number and took finding a parking place on the street as a good omen of what was to come.

Now that she'd located Charlotte's house, she felt a bit nervous. What if Charlotte was living with Lee? Or worse, what if Lee had brought Charlotte home and spent the night? She didn't want to embarrass anyone or cause a scene. She wanted to find a mutually satisfactory solution to both of their problems.

"Sitting in the car chewing on your fingernails isn't going to help anyone," she muttered. Opening the car door, she slid from under the steering wheel, stood and shut the car door. She coached herself, "What you're doing is best for everyone. You aren't selfishly jilting Lee. Whether he knows it or not, he must love Charlotte."

Out of habit, she glanced down at her white skirt, adjusted the trendy belt at her waist and fiddled with the gathered blue silk of her blouse that pleated beneath the belt. She wanted to appear calm and collected, even if her stomach did feel as though she'd had butterflies for breakfast.

She jabbed the doorbell button and waited. From inside the house she could hear a woman's high heels tapping on hardwood floors. The door opened the length that the chain lock allowed, giving Vanessa a quick glimpse of Charlotte.

The door slammed shut in Vanessa's face.

Undaunted, Vanessa punched the doorbell three times rapidly. "Charlotte, I've got to talk to you."

"Go away."

"Please, open the door. What I have to say is important to both of us."

"I don't want to talk to you. You're ruining my life, Lee's life. He doesn't love you. He loves me."

"I know. That's why I'm here."

"Do you take me for a fool? I know that all you have to do is tell him you talked to me and I'll never see him again."

Vanessa heard Charlotte sniffle. She rapped her knuckles on the wooden door frame. Determined not to leave without telling Charlotte how she felt, Vanessa rashly promised, "I won't tell Lee we've spoken."

She heard metal rasping against metal as Charlotte removed the safety chain from its holder. She knew the woman on the other side of the door was vainly trying to regain her composure before opening the door. This wasn't going to be any less difficult for Charlotte than it was for her. Silently she cursed Lee for putting both of them in such an awkward situation.

"Come in," Charlotte said, barely opening the door enough for Vanessa to squeeze through.

Vanessa's eyes scanned the homey atmosphere Charlotte had created in the parlor. Everything was immaculately clean, from the painted white woodwork to the highly polished top of the cocktail table in the living room. Muted blues and pale pinks blended harmoniously, from the walls to the chintz-covered sofa and chairs.

When her eyes moved back to Charlotte, she realized from the waitress uniform what Charlotte did for a living and that she must have been getting ready to go to work. She must have hastily dashed tears from her eyes, for traces of moisture clung to the tips of her lashes.

"Do you have time to talk for a few minutes?"

Charlotte nodded and gestured toward the parlor. "You're the last person in Charleston that I expected to see on my doorstep. We don't exactly run in the same circles."

Slightly offended by the implication that she was a snob, Vanessa said, "I'm guessing, but aren't we in the same business?"

"The Do-Come-Inn is a long way from The Butterfly... and I'm not talking about inches and feet."

"And I'm not here to discuss who belongs in what social circle. I'm aware the social strata in Charleston hasn't changed since the War Between the States, but love crosses those imaginary boundaries, doesn't it?"

"For some people, maybe, but not for Lee."

Vanessa thoughtfully digested that piece of information. Lee did strictly adhere to what he thought was proper, right from his wing-tipped shoes up to his Kennedy haircut. As far as she knew, Lee's only detour from the straight and narrow path of socially acceptable behavior was the woman who'd taken the seat across from her.

"Lee thinks you're the perfect woman for him." Charlotte's hands fluttered then settled on her lap, but not before she'd barely touched her rounded stomach. "You are."

Vanessa heard the pain in Charlotte's voice and knew what it cost her to make that statement. Instinctively Vanessa knew Charlotte's comment earlier hadn't been intended to hurt Vanessa.

Despite everything she'd ever heard or read about the other woman in a love triangle, Charlotte didn't fit the description. The other woman was supposed to be flashy, wearing tight clothes, sporting inch-long red-lacquered fingernails. Her voice should have been sultry, sexy. Her apartment was supposed to reek of exotic perfume and be decorated in sleazy satins.

The last thing a woman who was pregnant by another woman's fiancé should consider was how perfectly her lover suited his fiancée. It was obvious to Vanessa that Charlotte cared more for Lee than she did for herself. Momentarily she wondered if talking to Charlotte would have been easier if Charlotte had been bitchy.

Did Charlotte have to be so...nice? Vanessa couldn't help herself, she liked Charlotte. Under other circumstances, Charlotte would be the kind of woman Vanessa would have chosen as a friend.

She could understand why Lee had been drawn to Charlotte. Not only was Charlotte attractive, she fed his own belief that he could do no wrong. That had to be quite a male ego booster.

Lee would be getting far better than he deserved if he married Charlotte, Vanessa thought.

"Lee may think outward appearances are important, but I'm more concerned about who I am on the inside." Vanessa considered telling Charlotte that Lee was too shallow for either of them to be broken-hearted over, then thought again. Charlotte was blinded by love. Anything Lee said or did was the gospel truth in her eyes. To dispute Lee's viewpoint would only antagonize Charlotte. "Deep inside, I know that I don't love Lee and he doesn't love me."

"You don't love him?" From the wide-eyed expression on Charlotte's face she communicated her belief that Vanessa would be a fool not to love Lee. "You've gone together since kindergarten!"

"Not quite," Vanessa refuted. She wouldn't confuse the main issue by revealing her past history, but Vanessa knew that long before she'd been Lee's girlfriend, she'd tried to get Seth's attention. She'd failed back then; she hadn't failed last night. Thinking of Seth strengthened her resolve to right the wrong being done to Charlotte. "Last night I was on the landing above Lee's front door. From what I saw and heard, you're the one who should be marrying Lee on Saturday."

"You saw us?"

Vanessa observed a flush of mortification coloring Charlotte's face. In apology for causing Charlotte discomfort, she said, "I didn't mean to embarrass you. My being there was the best thing that could have happened for both of us."

"Lee wouldn't agree." Charlotte sadly shook her head. "He hates having his plans changed. We had another fight before I left him this morning."

From the increasing color in Charlotte's cheeks, Vanessa deduced that they'd made up in the same manner as the previous evening. If she and Seth made up afterward the way Charlotte and Lee did, Vanessa wouldn't mind having hourly confrontations. She concealed a wry grin by covering her mouth with her hand. Vanessa didn't want Charlotte to misconstrue the reason behind her smile as gloating over the difficulties Charlotte was having with Lee.

Vanessa asked, "Do you still want to marry him?"

"With all my heart," Charlotte replied without a moment's hesitation. Her eyes filled with tears as they met Vanessa's. "Otherwise, I'd have broken off our affair months ago. I've felt terrible about sneaking around behind another woman's back, but I couldn't stop myself. God knows I tried. I didn't know about you until it was too late."

"It's not too late for me to do something. Yesterday I tried to call off the wedding before I saw the two of you."

"Lee thinks you're having a bad case of prewedding jitters."

Vanessa openly grimaced. Did Lee share everything with Charlotte, including the nitty-gritty details of their relationship?

"I left a note under his door. Didn't Lee read it?"

"So that's what ticked him off this morning?" Charlotte said, smiling weakly. "I thought I'd done something to irritate him. This morning, he got up, went into the living room whistling, made a telephone call and came back to the, uh, came back in a bad mood."

Vanessa didn't need an architectural drawing of Lee's apartment to know where Charlotte had remained—snuggled in Lee's warm bed.

"That's when he told me I'd have to leave. He muttered something about his phone call and being sent out of town on business until Friday night," Charlotte concluded.

"So he really has gone," Vanessa mused aloud, disappointed.

So much for the well-rehearsed speech she'd intended to give Lee. She'd planned on soliciting Charlotte's help, then going straight to Lee's condo. From what Charlotte had just said, he had read her note but hadn't taken it seriously. He'd broken their luncheon date and accelerated the level of her prewedding jitters. Vanessa could almost visualize him reading her note, shrugging his shoulders and planning a showy apology. Did he really think sending dozens of roses and making himself unavailable would keep her from changing their wedding plans?

Mentally backtracking, Vanessa realized that he didn't know that she'd actually seen him with Charlotte. But regardless, he'd sadly underestimated her if he thought emptying the florists of their flowers and vanishing would manipulate her into marrying him.

"Yeah," Charlotte sighed after pausing. "I had high hopes that he wanted to spend his last few days of bachelorhood with me. When I begged him to let me go with him, I thought that was what infuriated him. You know how he is about business...business and pleasure don't mix."

Other than feeling certain Lee was a snob, Vanessa felt uncertain that she really knew anything else about Lee. It was a bit consoling to know she hadn't misread his attitude toward his job. Heaven knew, she'd been dead wrong about his ethics and morals.

Steering their conversation back on course, Vanessa said, "You don't seem pleased to know that I'm not marrying him."

"Lee's so all-fired determined to marry you that I think he'd drag you up the aisle and force you to say, 'I do.'" She paused thoughtfully. Her head jerked up as though she'd been struck with inspiration. "Unless..." She shook her head, obviously rejecting the idea.

"Unless...his...bride...was...willing?" Vanessa said, completing Charlotte's thought as though they were on the same wavelength. "You, not me?"

Both women stared at each other for a long moment, savoring the idea, weighing the pros and cons.

Vanessa mentally searched for things that could go wrong. The wedding rehearsal wouldn't be a problem. She'd pretend the flowers Lee sent excused him for breaking their luncheon date. She'd have to school her face into girlish submissiveness when she'd want to slap his, but she could do it, knowing a replacement would be standing in her shoes during the wedding ceremony.

She knew Lee would continue to avoid speaking to her privately, so she wouldn't have to worry about telling lies or keeping them straight. The tradition of the bride not seeing the groom on the wedding day would aid them in their plan. She'd make arrangements with the minister to dress at the church. She could give Charlotte her wedding dress, in case alterations were necessary, then take it to the church. On the morning of the wedding, she could keep everyone out of the dressing room while she helped Charlotte slip into the wedding dress.

What about walking down the aisle? Would the Colonel notice the switch? Not likely, she decided. He'd expect her to be nervous. All brides were nervous, weren't they? Charlotte could keep her head bowed and mutter yes and no answers to anything her grandfather asked.

"It wouldn't work," Charlotte apprehensively whispered. "He'd know."

"I don't think so," Vanessa responded thoughtfully. "At least not until you were beside him at the altar. We're about the same size. My veil has four layers of net. I can hardly see through it, which means he won't be able to see your face until you're up close."

"But even if I got that far, our marriage wouldn't be legal." Once again Charlotte paused. "Unless...unless the marriage license we got last month..."

"Don't clam up now! Have you and Lee had blood tests and everything?"

Lee shrank another notch in Vanessa's estimation. At his present rate of shrinkage, he would be able to spit and slide right underneath a door without any problem. Seth really would want to squash him under his heel if she told him about this!

"I forced him into it," Charlotte injected defensively. "I'd told him to get out of my life and stay out until he came back with a marriage license. A lot of good that did me. It's stored in my dresser drawer. You'll have yours hanging on your bedroom wall after Saturday."

"Wrong." Vanessa leaned forward as she warmed up to the idea. "Don't you see? Lee will be at the church, standing in front of all his friends and relatives. You walk up the aisle. He doesn't know who's behind the veil until you raise it. What can he do?"

"He wouldn't explode in front of his parents, his friends...his customers! He wouldn't want them to know that he'd been turned down."

"Right!" Vanessa concurred. "You know Lee better than I do. You tell me what he'll do."

Charlotte shook her head, grinning. "Marry me?"

"He'll do whatever it takes to save face," Vanessa finished, matching Charlotte's wide smile with one of her own. "In two shakes of a stick he'll straighten out the mix-up with the minister and thirty minutes later, you'll be married to him."

Elated at the prospect of Lee's character flaw causing his downfall, Vanessa chuckled. Poetic justice was far superior to revenge. And after all, wasn't Charlotte the woman he really should marry? she rationalized. So what if he was seething on the inside when Charlotte lifted the veil? Lee's anger might last until after the reception, but by the end of the honeymoon, he'd be glad Vanessa had switched places with Charlotte.

"But, Vanessa, what would all your friends say? You'd be the laughingstock of Charleston, wouldn't you?"

Touched by Charlotte's concern, Vanessa reached across the low cocktail table and patted Charlotte's hand. "Unless I'm mistaken, my friends that shielded me from finding out about Lee will be stunned by the switch, but they'll stick by me. And, if they don't, they weren't my friends to begin with. Don't worry about me."

Charlotte lifted her face toward the ceiling and rapidly blinked her eyelids to control her tears. "I was wrong about you. I thought you must be stuck-up because you're old-Charleston rich." A lone tear tracked down the side of her face. Self-consciously she swiped it away with the back of her hand. "Sometimes..." She gulped to keep from crying. "Sometimes, I've even hated you. One time I called the restaurant and asked for you. I was going to tell you all about Lee and me. I heard your voice and hung up, despising myself. You're helping me when you should be hating me. You have every right to hate me, too."

"I don't," Vanessa replied sincerely. "I'm not deluding myself into thinking I'm doing you a favor, either. I let myself drift into a relationship with Lee that was meaningless compared to what you feel for him. I'd have made him miserable. How long do you think it would have been before he was back on your doorstep? A month? A year? And now that I've seen the two of you together, I couldn't trust him. In the back of my mind, I'd always wonder if he wouldn't be happier with you. No, Charlotte, I don't hate you. Lee won't, either. You are the perfect woman for him."

Charlotte leaned forward and hugged Vanessa. Unchecked tears streamed down her face. "Just keep telling me that," she said, her voice hoarse with emotion. "I can't believe I'm going to be Mrs. Lee Hayden."

Vanessa squeezed her shoulders. "No time for tears. What time do you get off work?"

"Two o'clock."

"Fine. I have some other matters to take care of between now and then. I'll drop back by here around two-thirty with the gown and veil. Okay?"

"Oh, I just thought of something. What about the cost of the gown? The reception? I can't afford—"

"Consider it my wedding gift to you and Lee," she responded, raising both hands to quiet Charlotte's objections. "Lee's the one who wanted the big wedding."

"But—"

"No. I insist." Vanessa circled Charlotte's shoulders with one arm as she headed toward the front door. "Who knows, sometime in the near future I may borrow the gown back from you."

Genuine warmth shone in Charlotte's eyes as she said, "I hope you find someone to love you as much as I love Lee."

"I will. Drifting along isn't my style anymore. Back-peddling isn't, either. Next time I'll be setting my own course." While she spoke, she noticed the happiness in Charlotte's eyes fading. "What's wrong?"

"What's going to happen if Lee finds out about the switch before I walk down the aisle?"

"He won't. I imagine he plans on laying low until the wedding rehearsal Friday night. We'll figure out a way to get you into the balcony of the church without being seen, so you'll know what to expect Saturday. Since it's considered bad luck for the bride to take part in the rehearsal, he'll have little opportunity to speak to me privately."

"As long as we keep this between us, he won't find out. My lips are sealed," Charlotte promised, expecting a similar promise from Vanessa.

Vanessa hesitated before returning the promise. She'd formed a new alliance with Charlotte, but what about her other friendships? What about the Colonel? Seth? Gloria? Charles? Loyalty to her family and close friends struggled with her desire to help Charlotte.

She should tell the Colonel, she mused, but she knew him well enough to know how loud his initial reaction would be. Rifle shots and bombs dropping would be quiet in comparison. His military mind would consider Lee's betrayal akin to being a traitor. Traitors were shot, weren't they?

Also, she wanted to tell Seth. But, after what happened this morning, he wasn't going to believe partial explanations. He'd go after Lee and they'd be right back where they were years ago, with the police escorting Seth to a jail cell. Her grandfather had influenced the judge's decision once, but the Colonel might stick his cigar in his mouth and let Seth be sent to prison. Only this time, she wouldn't be the only one crying her heart out. Charlotte would be weeping in the background because their plan would have been spoiled.

"I've already told two people that I'm not marrying Lee," Vanessa confided. Watching Charlotte's bottom lip wobble, she added, "One of the two is a lifelong friend and the other...well, when Lee's roses arrived, he assumed I'd changed my mind once and had changed it back again."

"Will either of them talk to Lee?"

"If they did, I don't think they'd say anything he wanted to hear. Both Gloria and Seth are opposed to my marrying him."

"Then they'd be on my side, too, wouldn't they?" Her hand flew to her mouth. "Oh, dear, I don't mean that they would be disloyal to you by helping me. I meant that they wouldn't object to me marrying him?"

"No," Vanessa replied dryly. "But, knowing Gloria, I'll have to tell her what's going on or she'll be throwing a party to celebrate my being unengaged."

"And Seth doesn't believe you, so he shouldn't be a problem," Charlotte concluded. "What about your grandfather?"

Vanessa hated keeping secrets from the Colonel, but she didn't have a choice. He was the one person who could spoil the whole plan.

"My lips are sealed, too."

Seth licked the sample batch of icing from the tasting spoon. Sugar sweet, whipped cream smooth, he couldn't detect the small measurement of cream of tartar he'd added to the icing. Originally he'd planned on supervising the construction of the cake. It had been years since he'd done the actual grunt work in a kitchen. But he had changed his mind, thinking busy fingers would distract him from his inner turmoil. It hadn't.

He packed a sample from the regular sugar-based icing he had concocted into a pastry tube with the same force that a junkyard dog uses when sinking his teeth into a prowler's leg. He made two halfhearted attempts to form rose petals from the mixture before he slammed the tube onto the work counter. The icing made a burping noise as it spatted from the container onto the tiled floor.

Dammit, he groused silently, he wasn't going to let all the roses in South Carolina change Vanessa's mind.

One of the reasons he'd left New York and come to Charleston was to see Vanessa happily married. She wouldn't be happy with Lee. On the surface Lee Hayden looked like a blue-ribbon prize, but Seth knew that beneath Lee's Southern gentleman exterior was a ring-tailed polecat. Scratch Lee's hide and he'd stink to high heaven!

Seth grabbed the dish towel he'd flung over his shoulder and wiped up the mess he'd made. Wouldn't it be wonderful, he silently mused, if he could clean sticky-sweet Lee out of Vanessa's life as easily as cleaning up the icing mess he'd made? He tossed the towel onto the table and strode to the back door of the kitchen.

Morosely he realized he was back to the choice of telling Vanessa about Charlotte or keeping his mouth shut and praying for an earthquake to destroy the church before Saturday morning. He sensed that his prayers would go unanswered...nothing new for him. Sinners, albeit reformed, seldom had their prayers answered.

She won't thank you for telling her, he mused, staring at the glossy green magnolia leaves with unseeing eyes. Considering what had taken place between them last night, she might think he'd made up the whole story about Charlotte and Lee just to cause trouble. His present squeaky-clean behavior didn't change his reputation for being a troublemaker.

His thoughts strayed as his eyes focused on the courtyard where they'd made love. His skin could feel the touch of her hands, her lips. He rubbed his hands down the seams of his slacks, remembering how they'd felt on her bare skin. In the dark night, intimately entwined, there had been no doubts, no worries, only the marvelous enjoyment of discovering which sensitive places on her body brought her closer to the ultimate pleasure between a man and woman. He'd awakened her passion and introduced her into the sensual world.

She didn't have to be concerned about the physical side of their relationship being too platonic—it sizzled.

Eyes closing, he pictured her reaching up to him, wanting him as badly as he'd wanted her. Nothing in his life had been as perfect as making love with Vanessa.

Sure, he'd been with other women, but there had been a sameness about those experiences. Without love, sex boiled down to being a physical release for both the man and woman. It felt good to be caressed by a woman's hands; it felt glorious to be touched by the woman he loved. His brief comparison of other faceless women to Vanessa was like comparing drab moths to a colorful monarch butterfly—none measured up to her.

His eyes opened as a typical male insecurity surfaced. Had their lovemaking been terrific for Vanessa? Was the reason behind her changing her mind about not marrying Lee because he'd rushed her, wanted her too desperately to slow the pace?

He silently cursed himself for being so afraid of losing her that he'd made love in the grass rather than taking time to carry her to her bed.

His brow unwrinkled as he recalled trying to stop their lovemaking. She hadn't let him do the noble thing. She'd tasted the forbidden fruit and found it to her liking.

A small smile tilted the corners of his mouth upward. He felt fairly certain that whatever was behind Vanessa changing her mind wasn't because he'd been an unsatisfactory lover.

Call it conceit or confidence or whatever, deep down he knew the satisfaction he'd felt had been mutual.

He turned to one side as the sound of tires on the gravel leading to the carriage house drew his attention. Shortly after he'd turned his back on her and gone to the kitchen, he'd seen her car leaving. He wondered where she'd gone, but he'd been too busy struggling to keep control of his temper to ask Gloria.

It was too much to hope that she'd received Lee's flowers, gone to his apartment and told him to go straight to hell. Lee was smart. He'd patch up their quarrel.

Last night she'd been his, but he'd known even then that she was only meant to be his temporarily.

Heart thudding heavily in his chest, he knew his earlier decision to save her pride by not telling her about Lee's indiscretion was still the right one.

She didn't understand why there was a lack of passion between Lee and herself. Seth did. What he had to do was to convince Vanessa that what they'd shared was too good to ignore. Where Lee lacked passion toward her, Seth flamed with it.

In a slow jog, he started toward the carriage house garage, wondering if butterflies, like moths, were attracted to flames.

Seven

Head down as she followed the brick walkway into the courtyard, Vanessa contemplated how she was going to keep up the appearance of being a bride eagerly anticipating her wedding day. A lopsided grin tilted her mouth. Actually she was eager for Saturday morning to arrive. By noon Saturday, Charlotte would be Mrs. Lee Hayden; by midnight, Lee and Charlotte would be on their honeymoon. All she had to do in the meantime was keep up the appearance of being a willing bride, for Charlotte's sake.

Seth stopped, spread his feet apart and braced his legs to ready himself for the impact of Vanessa plowing into him. She was so absorbed in thought that he knew she hadn't noticed him.

Vanessa glanced up in time to stop, but didn't. Any

excuse for being caught in Seth's waiting arms was legitimate.

"Busy morning?" Seth asked, loving the feel of her arms circling his waist, her palms trekking up the taut flesh beside his spine.

"Productive."

Her reply didn't satisfy his curiosity to find out where she'd been, but her willingness to be loosely held in his arms in broad daylight assuaged his inner doubts. Sometimes body language spoke louder than words.

He nuzzled her hair, letting its silky texture and soft fragrance fill his senses. His hands tightened on her waist when she asked, "How was your morning?"

"An exercise in futility. I started working on the rose petals for the wedding cake."

Vanessa heard the frustrated tone in his voice, felt his fingers digging into her back. She longed to ease his mind by saying, "Don't bother. A wedding cake won't be necessary," but she'd promised Charlotte a wedding with all the trimmings, and that included a wedding cake, didn't it? How could she cancel the cake without everyone, including her grandfather and Charles, becoming suspicious?

She took a step backward, reluctantly letting her hands fall to her sides. "The wedding cake will be a work of art when you're finished."

The wedding was on again. Lee's roses and apology had been accepted, he deduced silently. She was graciously letting him down easy rather than openly telling him last night hadn't altered her plans.

Hurt, inwardly chafing to tell her that Lee wasn't good enough to lick her boots, Seth struggled to keep the expression on his face bland. Given a choice between champagne and beer, he couldn't blame her taste for the better things in life that she was used to having. Sidestepping off the path, he leaned one shoulder against an old oak.

Vanessa shoved her hands into her pockets to keep them from reaching toward him. His easygoing reaction perplexed her. The old Seth would have roasted her with his tongue for her behavior. He had every right to be mad as hell. What was wrong with him?

Her own temper flared at his casual dismissal of what had taken place between them. What kind of woman did he think she was to make love with one man and marry another three days later! Didn't he realize she'd given him something she'd never shared with another man? The very least he could do was try to convince her that she was making a grave mistake.

"You don't seem upset," she said, stating the obvious. "No recriminations?"

The hand behind his back raked against the rough bark of the tree, but he managed to maintain the illusion of having accepted her decision by shrugging. He'd come a long way from being the kid who'd been run out of town, but he still wasn't good enough for her. He swallowed hard, not trusting his voice to speak without betraying him.

Vanessa was tempted to hurl a few recriminations of her own in his direction or slap his face or…she didn't know what. *Dammit,* she silently blustered, *was last night just a one-night stand for him? Had what he'd said been a smooth line he'd perfected to get women into his bed?*

Her face flushed hotly as she realized her wanton response hadn't given him a chance to find a bed.

Monarch pride saved her. She wouldn't give Seth Kimble the satisfaction of knowing he'd hurt her. Her chin raised fractionally, and she forced a cordial smile to her lips as she said, "I've got a million things to do before the wedding. See you later."

The distance between the courtyard and the steps elongated into what seemed like a million miles. Her dignity measured the length of her stride—not too long, which would give the impression of fleeing, not too short, and seemingly reluctant to leave. Her ankles felt as though she'd strapped weights to them, but her dignity gave her the strength to keep her feet from shuffling on the brick path.

Once she reached her room, pride and dignity deserted her. She flung herself across her bed and let the tears she'd bottled flow freely.

Seth pushed against the tree with his hand to straighten and he winced. He glanced at his hand. Thin scratches sliced from the first knuckle of his fingers to the sensitive tips. The minor discomfort resulting from his self-inflicted injury was worth the price. He'd kept from hurting Vanessa by squealing on Lee. He'd managed to appear outwardly calm while being inwardly devastated. The tiny abrasions had given him the distraction he'd needed to maintain control of his temper, too.

Years ago, the mask of indifference he'd just adopted would have been impossible. He'd have verbally lashed into Vanessa, then gone in search of Lee to physically lash out at him. His stint in the military and the business world had taught him to govern his tongue and his fists.

The smell of cigar smoke alerted Seth to the Colonel's presence in the courtyard. Seth hadn't realized he'd been staring up toward Vanessa's room until he heard the Colonel speak.

"She'll make a beautiful bride, won't she?"

Seth felt the muscles in his shoulders tense at the frontal assault. The Colonel's watchful eye never missed anything that concerned the welfare of his granddaughter. Reminding Seth that shortly Vanessa would belong to another man was the Colonel's way of warning Seth to keep his eyes lowered to the ground and quit yearning for the moon.

"Yes, she's beautiful," Seth agreed, refusing to be goaded.

"There was a time when I was worried about her future, but after Saturday her future will be in Lee's capable hands."

Seth saw the Colonel's bushy eyebrows raise as his cigar shifted to the left side of his mouth. Smoke clouded the air between them. If the movements were intended to intimidate, Seth negated their effect by replying, "You trained Vanessa well. She's capable of taking care of herself, with or without a husband."

"Humph! I'm old-fashioned enough to think a woman hasn't found her niche in life until she's established in her own home, with her own man to take care of her."

"In that case, you should have married her off the minute she graduated from high school."

"I tried; she balked. I taught her to think for herself, to be independent. When I tried to do her thinking for her, she politely told me that she wasn't ready to get married." Thaddeus removed the cigar from his mouth and flicked the ash. "Independence is a double-edged sword. It cuts both ways."

The Colonel's admission that he was unable to make Vanessa march to his tune struck Seth as being odd. In fact, now that he thought about it, the Colonel chatting with him was damned peculiar. The old man never made a move without the forethought necessary for a major military invasion.

The Colonel's behavior was growing more and more curious. He was talking in circles, getting nowhere. Bemused, Seth watched him drop his cigar onto the ground and grind it out with the heel of his shoe.

"Damned cigars aren't what they used to be," Thaddeus grumbled. "Nothing is like it used to be."

"In some cases that's a blessing."

"It's a blessing where you're concerned. I've been keeping a close eye on you. You've changed."

Flattery coming from the Colonel increased Seth's curiosity about the Colonel's mysterious behavior. "I'm older, if that's what you mean."

The Colonel thumped his fist on his heart then tapped his finger to his forehead. "I mean in here...and here. You had a chip on your shoulder from the day the social worker dropped you at our back door."

"Most youngsters know when they aren't welcome," Seth replied candidly.

"That was your mother's fault. She broke Charles's heart when she refused to..." Realizing he'd said more than he'd intended and was raking over cold ashes that were best forgotten, he made a production of finding another cigar. He rummaged in his outside jacket pockets, his breast pockets and his shirt pocket. "Must have left them inside."

Seth knew Thaddeus was looking for an excuse to make a hasty retreat, so he halted the Colonel by finishing his sentence. "Stay married to him? To give Charles custody of me?"

"Who told you that? Your mother?"

"The social worker who brought me here after my mother died."

"Hogwash! Charles and your mother fought, but it sure as hell wasn't over who was going to get custody. Charles was crazy about her. He did everything humanly possible to hold their marriage together."

"Then why'd he walk out?" Seth fought against letting the old feelings of being unloved and unwanted wash over him. He thought he'd outgrown the need to gain the Colonel's approval, but old habits died hard. "I thought in your good old days a man stuck by his wife and child."

"Mister, you're talking desertion?" Thaddeus thundered. He stooped down, picked up the remains of his cigar, broke off the smashed end and rammed the butt into his mouth. "Are you man enough to take the truth plain and simple?"

Seth nodded. Automatically his body tensed as though waiting for a solid blow. He'd waited a long time for answers about his mother and father's relationship. Throughout his late childhood and teenage years, Charles had refused to answer any and all questions regarding his mother.

"She married Charles because she was pregnant."

The bombshell the Colonel thought he'd dropped left Seth unfazed. An untimely pregnancy was no excuse for raising a child without love. "So what? That happens to a lot of women."

"But most women don't tell the man they've just married that the child she's carrying isn't his." Thaddeus glanced toward the discarded remains of his cigar. He bent down and began fieldstripping the portion he'd thrown into the grass as he spoke. "Your dad was a good-looking fellow, but she made it crystal clear that she'd set her sights on a man who'd graduated from the U.S. Naval Academy. She told Charles he wasn't good enough for her. After you were born, she used to taunt Charles by saying that only a fool would marry a woman who was carrying another man's child. When Charles got a bellyful of her flagrantly running wild and cheating on him, he walked out. Yes, he deserted you, but with good cause. To this day, he doesn't know for certain whether or not you're his son."

"And yet he raised me? Why? Why didn't he put me in foster care? Or send me to military school? He must have felt like throwing up every time he looked at me."

"He loved you. Love can be a double-edged sword, too. It can bring joy or sorrow."

An insight previously denied Seth hit him squarely between the eyes. The Colonel thought he was legally a bastard. That wasn't a social handicap now, but it was thirty years ago. They'd all known he was a bastard child, and he'd fulfilled their belief by acting like one.

Appearance-wise, Seth knew he resembled his mother. Action-wise, he'd certainly inherited the wild streak from his mother's side of the family. To the Colonel, Seth had never been Charles's son and never could be. In Charleston, being a bastard was the closest thing possible to committing the original sin. Bloodlines were everything that determined who a man was and what he'd become.

Seth also presumed that neither the money he'd earned, nor the reputation he'd gained in the food industry could remove the tarnish of his birth. As far as the Colonel was concerned, Seth still wasn't good enough for his granddaughter.

And yet, Seth had the gut feeling that the Colonel wanted him to prove he was Charles's son. Why? If Vanessa's grandfather wanted to bring him to his knees, why was he so damned nervous about doing it?

Because he's testing you, Seth conjectured. He wants to know the effect his bombshell has on your self-confidence. He wants to know your weaknesses, your vulnerabilities. He knows you don't have Lee Hayden's impeccable background, but he's still worried about you and his granddaughter.

"I won't apologize for my lack of pedigree," Seth said quietly, offering the Colonel his hand to steady his balance as the Colonel rose to his feet. The Colonel wasn't the only one who'd kept a close surveillance on the happenings at The Butterfly. Seth had been watching, too, and discovered a few kinks in the Colonel's armor. When they were eye to eye, Seth added, "There are other double-bladed swords in life besides independence and love."

It was the Colonel's turn to ask, "Such as?"

"Generosity. I grew up thinking that your letting Charles and I live under your roof was an act of charity on your part. It wasn't, was it? You needed Charles as much as he needed you. I've been in enough restaurants to know that competent chefs are few and far between. Restaurants are a dime a dozen. I wonder what would happen to The Butterfly if Charles had the wherewithal to open a place of his own?"

"Charles has been with me for over twenty years. This is his home. He wouldn't consider leaving The Butterfly to work elsewhere."

The look of dismay on the Colonel's face was enough to make any underdog sit up and howl with delight. The Colonel was worried about losing his chef and his granddaughter to the rogue he'd had run out of town.

A lesser man would have responded differently, but Seth magnanimously said, "You're right. Charles does consider this his home."

"Definitely *his* kitchen. He's the one who draws the line outside the kitchen door, not me."

"He has his domain, you have yours. Separate but equal. You've treated him fairly."

"Are you implying that I haven't always been fair with you?"

"Have you?"

Thaddeus stared hard at Seth before removing the unlit cigar from his mouth and answering, "If you're referring to my having a private word with the judge before he rendered a decision, let me say this. Under the same set of circumstances, I'd still use my influence to get you into the military forces." He dug into his pants pocket until he found a wooden match. Raking the red tip against the bark of the oak, he squinted up at Seth as he puffed on his cigar stub until it was lit. "Like I said, though, things have changed. You may think I'm a stubborn old man who's set in his ways, but I'm not too blind to see or too senile to learn. I've been watching you. I'd say offhand that you had a reason for coming back here, and it wasn't to bake a wedding cake."

"There was," Seth admitted. "I wanted to make peace with my father...."

"And?"

"And to see Vanessa happily married." Seth measured his words carefully. "Personally, I don't think Lee Hayden will make her happy." That wins the understatement-of-the-year award, Seth tacked on silently. Vanessa would be heartbroken once she found out about Lee's long-term involvement with another woman.

Thaddeus thumped his cigar with his ring finger. His head thoughtfully bobbed up and down. "I told her that she doesn't have to marry Lee as far as I'm concerned. I can't quite put my finger on what it is about Lee that bothers me, but he reminds me of a fellow I met during the big war. This guy looked as American as apple pie—blond hair, blue eyes, tall—and he talked like a Yankee who had a family history that went back to the Mayflower." Holding the stub between his thumb and forefinger, Thaddeus put the cigar in his mouth. His eyes locked with Seth's eyes. "He fooled darned near all of us. He turned out to be one of Hitler's spies who'd infiltrated behind our lines. No telling how many lives he cost us."

From what the Colonel had said and the look in his eyes, Seth discerned what was behind the smoke screen. Colonel Monarch knew all about Lee Hayden.

"Have you told Vanessa of your doubts?"

The Colonel dryly chuckled and said, "I try not to wander blindly through the same mine field twice. Look what happened when I discouraged her from idolizing you. She followed you around like you were personally responsible for making the sun rise every morning." He exhaled a steady stream of smoke away from Seth's face. "No, I haven't told Vanessa about my suspicions. She'd defend Lee—probably marry him just to prove me wrong. Loyalty cuts both ways, too."

"Yeah," Seth agreed. "I'll wager the whole town loves Vanessa too much to hurt her by saying anything against Lee."

"You'd win your bet."

Mentally Seth jumped one step ahead of the Colonel. "You need an outsider to do the dirty work. Mc?"

"The thought had crossed my mind, but I quickly laid it to rest. Vanessa needs a man who's worthy of her. Someone who can pull himself up by his bootstraps and march forward at the same time."

"Who?" Seth asked, wondering who the Colonel had chosen as a replacement.

"You. You could marry her."

Seth felt as though the Colonel had completely outflanked him. One minute he was giving him the harsh facts surrounding his birth and the next, he was suggesting the illegitimate son of the restaurant's chef marry his granddaughter.

Waving his hand toward the mansion, Seth said, "I can't give Vanessa anything compared to this."

"What can you give her? Love? Can anyone love her more than you?"

"No."

"Would you purposely do anything to make her unhappy?"

"No."

"Would you marry her for her money or her social position?"

"No."

"Could she trust you?"

"Yes."

The Colonel made a chopping motion with his hand and said, "Then completely sever yourself from the kid you used to be. You're the man she needs. And unless I'm way off mark, you're the man she loves."

Seth gave the Colonel a hard look. "What makes you say that?"

"The sparkle in her eyes. The way she looks at you when she thinks no one is watching. In case you haven't noticed, she's downright protective of you. To the point of waging war with me." Thaddeus sucked on the chewed end of his cigar. "I know my grand-daughter. She's cooking up something."

As the Colonel spoke, Seth's face broke into a genuine smile.

"She's a lousy cook," the Colonel said with a gri-mace. "A great restaurant manager, mind you, but she needs a gourmet chef to help her carry out her plans. Like I said, I'm not blind or senile . . . just slow in my old age. I should have had this talk with you the day you arrived." He clamped his hand on Seth's shoul-der, then extended his hand in the age-old gesture of friendship. "Yes, sir, I should have. I sincerely hope I'm not waving the white flag too late. Truce?"

Seth quickly mulled over the Colonel's confession in his mind. He'd readily admitted to past and present attempts to maneuver men in and out of Vanessa's life. He'd admitted to being prejudiced against Seth. Those two items came as no surprise. What did surprise Seth was the Colonel conducting truce talks with him. It shouldn't have. War makes strange bedfellows. The Colonel wasn't surrendering Vanessa to him; he was only enlisting reinforcements.

"Truce."

Seth took his hand. The Colonel's grip was as strong as a man half his age. Neither Seth nor Thaddeus tried to bust the other man's knuckles. Eyes meeting, they silently communicated their common mission: get rid of Lee Hayden.

Vanessa stood at her bedroom window and watched her grandfather and Seth shake hands. Anxiously she wondered if their handshake was the standard male ritual that came before both men started swinging. Given the differences in their ages and physical stature, she knew who'd have the advantage, but she also knew Seth would never strike her grandfather. Even in extreme circumstances, Seth treated the Colonel with utmost respect.

Giving her nose a final swipe with a tissue, she watched them peacefully separate, going in opposite directions. The Colonel, puffing on his infernal cigar, slowly moved toward the front sidewalk. Seth briskly headed toward the kitchen. She willed Seth to turn around, to look up, to come to her, but her mental telepathy failed.

She wadded the damp tissue into a ball and tossed it into the waste can. She'd spent the past half hour feeling sorry for herself and it hadn't helped one iota. Come to think of it, less than a week ago, she'd been standing in exactly the same spot bemoaning the fact that she'd avoided emotional upheaval by drifting into an unsatisfactory relationship with Lee. Moaning and groaning hadn't helped then, either.

Seth Kimble's arrival had been the catalyst that had dramatically changed her. He'd reentered her life and turned it inside out, upside down and sideways. Her restrictive cocoon no longer felt safe and secure. It felt binding, suffocating. Fully aware of the dangers of emerging from her cocoon, she had made one snap decision after another, diving into an emotional whirlpool headfirst. She'd decided to confront Lee. After discovering Lee's passionate relationship with Charlotte, she'd made love with Seth. Then she'd impulsively decided to help Charlotte become Mrs. Lee Hayden.

She didn't regret the radical changes she'd made. She did regret the necessity for keeping her mouth shut. Nothing would have given her greater pleasure than to have announced her change in plans to Seth and the Colonel.

"Gloria." Vanessa whispered the name of the one person unrestricted by her vow of silence. She'd need help to carry this off without being discovered. Later, she silently promised, she'd show Seth that she wasn't fickle.

Vanessa checked both the kitchen and the dining room to make certain Charles and the Colonel were too busy to notice she was missing. She scampered across the courtyard and climbed the wooden steps to the upper story of the carriage house.

Earlier she'd devoted her energies to finalizing her plans with Gloria and Charlotte. Friday night at the wedding rehearsal she'd be the bride. Saturday morning Charlotte would replace her. She'd shocked Gloria, her matron of honor, into complete speechlessness when she'd asked her not to reveal Charlotte's identity until the veil was lifted. Enthralled by the chance to play a part in giving Lee his comeuppance, Gloria had begun babbling about how happy Seth would be to know that Vanessa was free. Vanessa had had to extract a promise from Gloria she wouldn't tell anyone—Seth included—both to protect Charlotte and to ensure that their scheme would go without a hitch. The thought that something might go wrong prodded Gloria to seriously accept Vanessa's terms.

No, she thought silently as she quietly rapped on Seth's screen door, she'd been wise to handle this situation her way.

She knocked harder when Seth didn't respond. He was there. The lights were on and the outside door wasn't shut. She opened the screen and entered, calling, "Seth?"

From the back of the good-size apartment she heard the shower running and a male voice singing slightly off-key. Two seconds and a mischievous smile later, Vanessa was striding down the narrow hallway toward the guest bath. Should she go in? Feeling delightfully wicked, which wasn't typical of her normal behavior, she removed one shoe, then the other, and pushed open the door.

Steam filled the small room, making it hot and sultry, fogging the mirror with dampness. The combination of the frosted glass enclosure and steam concealed more of Seth's back than it revealed. She could barely see in; therefore, Seth couldn't see her either, she decided, lowering the toilet seat and perching herself on it.

She covered her mouth to stop from giggling when the Barry Manilow love song he'd been singing switched to a bawdy military marching tune. What he lacked in vocal ability was made up for in volume and enthusiasm.

"Whooee!" Seth exclaimed, turning off the hot water. An icy stream of cold water sprayed over his body. Gritting his teeth to keep them from chattering, he wondered how many more frigid showers he'd have to endure.

He'd mapped out several new strategies since talking to the Colonel and Charles. He asked his father for his opinion on whether or not he objected to his son actively pursuing the boss's daughter, after they'd cleared the murky water surrounding their relationship.

Seth scrubbed his hands and arms as he recalled the strained silences that had marked their discussion. It hadn't been easy. Charles felt uncomfortable talking about his ex-wife because he'd strictly adhered to his belief that the less said about her, the better. In the final analysis Charles summed his feelings up by simply saying, "You're my son. I'm part of who you are and what you've become. You're mine."

And then he'd chewed Seth out royally for doubting his own self-worth. At least his son could tell the difference between the flavor of nutmeg and cloves. Vanessa was a little sweetheart and Charles vowed that he dearly loved her, but she certainly needed someone in her life to keep her spice rack in order.

Seth grinned at his father's analogy. The grin widened as he recollected Charles's suggestion to kidnap her en route to the church.

Kidnapping Vanessa before the wedding appealed to Seth. Mentally he could picture her dressed in her wedding gown, tossed over his shoulder and heading toward the airport. He hoped Lee would try to stop him.

"Twin tire tracks straight up his tuxedo," Seth sang merrily. "Move 'em out, move 'em out. Go to your left, your right..."

Seth rinsed the part of his body that was giving him the most trouble whenever he saw Vanessa, then his face. He opened the shower door. Blindly he reached for the towel rack.

Vanessa grinned. Leaning forward, she pushed the towel toward his hand, asking, "Can I be of assistance?"

"Vanessa?" Seth grabbed the towel and slung it low on his hips. Cold showers weren't what they were cracked up to be. He wasn't ashamed of his automatic physical reaction to hearing Vanessa's voice, but he didn't want to step from the shower with the towel blatantly tented in front of him, either.

"Were you expecting some other woman?" Vanessa teased. She blinked her eyes rapidly as though they'd work like windshield wipers and would clear her vision.

"Several," he retorted, chuckling. "I got used to group showers while I was in the service."

"Is that right? Coed service—coed showers?" She knew he was kidding, but that didn't stop a flash of jealousy from prompting her into swinging the door wide open and stepping inside. Brazenly she looped her arms around his wet shoulders and added, "I'm surprised you didn't sign up for another four-year hitch."

Seth could feel his towel slipping downward. Any good intentions he'd had about keeping his hands off Vanessa until she promised to marry him slid right along with his towel.

"The showers were great, but the food was lousy. Besides, a man who's forced into the military isn't likely to re-up."

Eight

Slowly, with one hand, Seth reached for the handle of the cold water faucet, and with the other hand he shifted Vanessa until she was directly beneath the shower's nozzle. From the way her hips had naturally cradled against his, he knew he wasn't the only one in need of an icy blast of cold water.

Vanessa ran her thumb around the dark brown orb of his nipple, intent on learning what aroused him. Just watching his reflexive response made her nipples grow taut with desire. Her lips closed over the tip as she wondered what reaction that would cause.

Seth twisted his hand clockwise. Frigid water blasted from the nozzle.

"Seth!"

Before she could recover her wits and retaliate, Seth stepped out of the shower and held the door shut. It was a dirty trick that ranked right up there with being awakened by having your big toe pulled out of its socket, but it had saved him from forcefully evicting Vanessa from the shower stall or giving in to the rush of desire threatening to impair his thought processes.

Instantly soaked to the skin, Vanessa pivoted around and turned off the water. She tugged on the door. "Have you lost your ever-lovin' mind?"

"No," Seth chuckled. "I just avoided instant insanity. Your hands were driving me crazy."

Vanessa glared at his shadow blocking the exit and swiped her hair back from her face. "Can't you talk your way out of a corner? Did you have to get physical?"

"I was talking. You weren't listening."

Silently conceding him the point, she reached her hand over the stall door and asked, "Do you have an extra towel?"

The only towel close enough to reach was around his hips, and he wasn't about to relinquish that one. In the second it took to cross to the linen closet, Vanessa burst out of the shower stall. Pure devilry was in her eyes as she stalked him backward.

Seth's eyes followed the rivulets of water from her hair down to the white blouse plastered against her breasts. Wet, the fabric outlined her puckered nipples. Desire stabbed him.

"Very funny, Mr. Kimble." She saw his eyes hungrily glued to her chest, and his wistful smile. She reached out and snatched the closest towel available, leaving Seth completely nude. "A cold shower didn't lower your thermostat, did it?"

"No, but it lowered yours, changing you from a hot seductress to an icy termagant." Nudity didn't embarrass Seth; his uncontrollable reaction to her close proximity did. Clenching his teeth until his back molars ground together, he decided he wasn't going to allow wanting her to interfere with finding out why she'd decided to practice her womanly wiles on him.

Oh so casually he sauntered from the bathroom door into the adjoining bedroom. He retrieved his worn jeans from the closet and tugged them up his damp legs. A zip and a snap later, he said, "Dry off and we'll talk."

From the go-to-hell look in her eyes, Seth wondered if she'd ever speak civilly to him again. Seth glanced away, knowing the hunger gnawing at his insides was clearly reflected in his eyes. Wet straggly hair, defiant eyes, damp clothing and all, he still wanted her.

Vanessa's mind was spinning faster than an egg beater. The look she'd seen in his eyes had cooled her temper a fraction. The tiny mole she'd seen on his posterior wasn't a wart, and yet it reminded her of a time when they'd joked about it. Anger, passion and laughter swirled through her mind as she closed the door, stripped out of her soggy clothes, located a dry towel and wrapped it around herself.

"What about the wedding?" Seth called through the door as he closed the drapes and turned on the bedside lamp.

Honoring her oath of silence, Vanessa evasively asked, "Do you think I'd be here attempting to seduce you if I was going to marry Lee Hayden?"

"Good question."

Seth folded himself into the armchair beside the bed and waited for her to come out of the bathroom.

Vanessa fluffed a towel across her limp hair. "That wasn't what he was supposed to say," she mouthed at her reflection in the mirror. When she'd mentally gone through this discussion in her own bathroom, she'd had Seth simply reply, "No." Then she wouldn't say anything and he'd sweep her into his arms. Love scene . . . big time.

Stubbornly refusing to let her original plan go awry, she tried again to stuff words into his mouth. "Are you questioning my principles?"

Seth smiled to cover the pang of hurt he felt when she stressed the words *you* and *my*. From the tone of her voice he gathered that she considered her principles above reproach, but his were down and dirty.

"It wouldn't be the first time I've been victimized by the principles of a Monarch."

Loyal to the marrow, Vanessa swung the bathroom door open. By raising one eyebrow, she silently demanded to know exactly what he meant.

"The Colonel didn't have any qualms about influencing a judge without bothering to find out if I was guilty."

Vanessa quickly made a turban of the towel she'd used to dry her hair and crossed to the corner of the bed. She'd heard her grandfather's side of the story. She wanted to hear Seth's version.

Swallowing hard, Seth watched her walking toward him. The intimacy of having her in his bedroom clothed only in bath towels tested his self-control. It would take an ounce of strength to remove the towel; it took pounds of restraint to remain seated.

"Were you guilty?" she asked, perching on the bed.

"Of car theft, no—of stupidity, yes."

He gripped the arms of the upholstered chair to keep from making another dumb move. In the back of his mind he kept thinking about how she looked, how she'd feel underneath him, how she'd taste. He knew he had to open up the past before they could advance into the future. Knowing what had to be done and doing it, he discovered, were poles apart.

"Anyone knows it's dumb to go joyriding with a kid having parent problems. I didn't furnish the car or the booze, but two hours later, I was arrested for car theft." Seth grimaced, remembering how asinine he'd felt. "The car belonged to the other kid's parents. Since I was known as the Charleston hellion, his parents decided I was a bad influence on their son, so they wouldn't drop the charges."

"The Colonel told me that you went into the service and the other guy was shipped off to college." The injustice of the situation was twice as bad as she'd conjectured. Not only was Seth harshly punished, but he hadn't committed a crime. Her heart went out to him. She'd have given anything to have been able to step back in time and change the course of events.

Seth leaned forward in his chair, drawn toward the compassion he heard in her voice. "It appears we've both had a long talk with your grandfather. Did the Colonel also tell you that I'm a bastard?"

"Talked? For him to call you names, you must have come close to getting physical with him."

"No, Vanessa. I'm not speaking figuratively. According to what my mother told Charles shortly after they were married, Charles isn't my father."

"Then who is?"

Seth dismissed the importance of who his biological father was by raising one shoulder.

"Does Charles know?"

"I haven't asked. Oh, yes, I've considered asking Charles, but I decided against it."

Seth moved beside her onto the bed. He needed for her to understand how it felt to be exiled and why he couldn't hurt Charles.

"I was bitter when I left here. I swore I'd never return. And yet, there wasn't a week that passed when I didn't think about someone or something here. In my mind I compared every charming restaurant with The Butterfly. I compared weather, oceans, people—everything. Home. Nostalgia. Nothing measures up to it. Funny how bitter memories can become unbearably sweet."

Vanessa kept quiet. She wanted to open her arms and draw him to her chest to assuage his hurt. By disclosing his innermost feelings, his vulnerabilities, she knew he was going beyond the physical attraction they felt for each other. He was sharing what was in his heart and soul.

"The letter I received from Charles that asked me to return was like an exile being asked to return home. I don't think I'll ever forget the expression on his face when we talked about my restaurant. I felt vindicated, exonerated for all the petty offenses I did commit."

Seth was unaware he'd been clenching his hands together, until they ached. Vanessa lightly touched his wrist, easing his tension, allowing him to relax his bone-crushing grip.

"Charles is proud of me. To take that away from him would be worse than theft. I'd be stealing another man's pride and joy. I can't do that just to satisfy my curiosity."

Vanessa felt her heart brimming with love for the man beside her. He personified every value she held dear: loyalty, honor, trustworthiness. Now a lot of things she hadn't understood made sense. Because of the shadow surrounding his birth, Charles had been unable to be openly affectionate with Seth. Like any other boy, Seth had needed Charles's attention. When the man he thought was his father couldn't give him love, Seth had gotten attention from everyone by becoming a rebel.

"I loved you," she murmured. She took his hand and placed it on her heart. "I couldn't express my love any better than Charles did, but I cared. I love you now more than I thought humanly possible."

Seth felt her heart pounding steadily beneath his hand. Her eyes shimmered with love. "Then you can't marry Lee. I won't let you," Seth said.

"Kiss me, Seth," she pleaded, her promise to Charlotte weighing heavily on her heart. Seth was a physical man. He'd understand her silence if only he'd touch her.

"I want to." His fingers traced over the edging of the towel, lingering at the place where she'd tucked it together. "God knows I want you more than the air I breathe, but I can't make love to you. I've always had a part-time kind of love. I can't settle for left-overs . . . not with you.''

Vanessa was caught in a dilemma of her own making. Love and loyalty warred silently in her mind. She couldn't tell Seth of Charlotte's plan without going into the details of who Charlotte was and why she was helping her. Once Seth found out that Lee had been unfaithful to her, she knew he wouldn't be able to control his temper.

Vainly she searched for a compromise. She'd counted on Seth physically wanting her too much to demand an explanation. He did want her, but he wouldn't jeopardize a lasting love with sexual gratification. She had to ask him for the one thing she wasn't certain he was capable of giving.

"Trust me? Just this once, have faith in me that I'll do what's right for both of us?"

"Blind trust," Seth muttered, uncertain he was capable of completely trusting anyone.

Hearing the wariness in his voice, she replied, "Yes. Trust. It's the cornerstone of love."

Seth felt a flash of childhood panic. He'd been forced to rely only upon himself. She was asking for more than his love. She was asking him to relinquish the control it had taken for him to make his own fate. Figuratively he'd be handing his heart over to her to do with as she chose.

His survival instincts raged to the forefront of his mind, issuing a loud warning: Trust her and you'll have nothing left if she betrays you.

A wry smile raised one side of his mouth. Loving her the way he did, he wouldn't be worth a damn without her anyway. He had to trust her.

"I love you," he succumbed, his mouth hovering over hers. Her eyes gazed back steadily at him. He loved her more than he'd loved anyone, anything. She was everything he'd ever wanted and had never been able to have. "I'm yours. I'll die loving you."

He brushed his mouth against hers, almost afraid of physically relinquishing his soul by passionately kissing her. Her soft moan and the feel of her tongue tracing the crease of his lips exploded a rush of desire through him that left him trembling.

Vanessa pressed against him. Her tongue slid into the sweetness of his mouth. Had she been aware of his thoughts, she'd have tasted victory. But she only tasted pure love. His tongue rasped beneath hers, enticing her to know him inside and out.

Seth used the primitive strength that so worried Vanessa to gently lower her shoulders to the pillow. The flimsy knot in her towel parted without his assistance. Vanessa clung to his lips, pulling him on top of her. Without ending the kiss, he agilely removed his jeans and sank into her softness. His blunt fingers moved over her breasts, her slender waist, the womanly flair of her hips and back up again.

She bunched his longish damp hair in her fingers as he deepened her kiss. Her hands pressed them together as she stroked his shoulders, following the indentation of his back down to the small imperfection that blemished his buttocks. His skin was hot. Her palms were damp from touching his hair, and inside,

Vanessa was sizzling. Her fingers dug into the pads of muscles covering his bones.

Seth groaned as their lips parted, his breath rasping in his throat. He felt her leg rubbing against his, silk against sandpaper. His mouth trailed down to the feminine swell of her breast. His hands cupped her breasts, forming a luscious valley in which he buried his face.

Vanessa arched her back in pleasure as he moved his lips to the tip of her breast. Unconsciously her fingers tightened in his hair. Seth mouthed her nipple more forcefully, drawing it deeper into his mouth. A tingling sensation shot from her breast to the achy juncture of her legs.

"Oh, Seth!" she gasped, feeling a hot flood of desire making intelligible speech impossible.

From the one time they'd made love, he'd learned how sensitive her breasts were. She was as greedy for his touch as he was to touch her. Slowly, fiercely, tenderly, he disciplined his mouth and hands to give her the utmost pleasure. The suction of his lips became increasingly demanding as she moved beneath him. His breathing became labored, hard and heavy.

"Enough," she implored, afraid she'd reach her peak without him. She moved her legs apart, silently pleading for him to take her.

Seth filled her with one hard stroke. This time he didn't have to worry about hurting her. His movements were strong, primitive, bordering on savage when she wrapped her legs around his hips and clenched her thighs. She moved with him, her eyes wild, shining with the pleasure of her passion.

Her eyes squeezed tightly shut as she valiantly tried to stall the minor explosions within her body. There was no containing them. She cinched her legs around Seth, savored the feelings, then gave way as the sensation of shattering into a million sparkling pieces enveloped her.

Seth simultaneously exploded. He collapsed into her arms, trusting her, loving her, too spent to worry about losing her.

"You can trust me to drive you to the wedding rehearsal," Seth informed Vanessa, voice lowered, teeth clenched. "I won't wreck your car."

Trust, trust, trust. From bacon and eggs this morning, through turkey club sandwiches at lunch and scampi at dinner, he'd fed her a steady diet of things she could trust him to do. The closer they came to the wedding rehearsal, the more often she heard it.

She'd been within minutes of departing for the church when Seth had entered her room unannounced and offered to be her chauffeur.

Intuitively she knew the blind trust he'd given her was wearing thinner than a French crepe. He wanted reassurance that she wasn't going to marry Lee. She wanted to tell him not to worry, that she had everything in control, but she knew she'd be wasting her breath. As far as Seth knew, her plans hadn't changed.

"That's sweet of you to offer to drive me to the church, Seth, but I heard Charles say he'd be alternating between the kitchen and the dining rooms. You don't have to suffer through the rehearsal. Why don't you stay here and help Charles?"

"Charles doesn't need my help. You can rely on me to get you there safely."

"I have faith in your driving ability. It's your temper I'm worried about," she replied honestly. "You've been following me around today looking like a time bomb waiting for the hand to strike zero."

Seth couldn't deny her accusation. As each minute ticked by, he'd felt closer and closer to detonation. Only by staying away from her, other than at meals, had he been able to keep his temper under control. Fighting with her was the last thing he wanted to do.

"What'd you expect? We're only hours away from the wedding!"

Smiling, Vanessa nodded. Everything was set. Gloria had helped Charlotte with the minor alterations on the wedding gown. The honeysuckle flower arrangements had arrived at the church. The gifts she'd received from her friends and distant relatives had been repacked, ready for shipment. Other than Seth being a problem, her day had been busy and fruitful.

"You said you trusted me," she reminded.

"Right up to the part in the ceremony where you say, 'I do'? You're asking for more than blind trust. You're asking me to dig a hole and throw the dirt back in on myself."

"Please, Seth," she said, begging for a few hours more of trust. "Tomorrow you'll understand."

"You won't explain?"

"I can't explain." She tossed her purse into the car to free both of her hands. Placing them on Seth's forearms, she looked him straight in the eye and said, "I love you."

"Are you going to leave Lee standing at the altar?"

"I love you."

"Are you going to get up there and say no?"

"I love you."

Seth dragged her into his arms, crushing her against his chest. "I'm scared, Vanessa. You're everything I've ever wanted. I do trust you, but not knowing what's going to happen is pure hell."

Hugging him fiercely, Vanessa sorely regretted her promise to Charlotte. Her fingers dug into the back of his white shirt until they left small dents in the fabric.

She raised on tiptoe, releasing her hold on his shirt and pulling his head down with her hands. Her kiss would have to restore his faith in her. He had to trust her.

Seth ground his lips against hers. Whatever secret she was keeping, he'd been unable to unlock her lips with questions. She tasted sweet, so damnably sweet.

"Go," he whispered, his breathing ragged. "I'll drive the Colonel to the church."

An hour later, Vanessa sat in the first pew of the church, knowing how the Colonel must have felt when he'd been put in charge of a full-scale military operation—only her troops were threatening to go AWOL. Seth and the Colonel had joined forces and were seated in the back pew, scowling at her. Lee was at the front of the church, grinning smugly. Charlotte was in the balcony and Gloria was flitting between them like Greta Garbo auditioning for a role in a major film as a counterintelligence spy.

She glanced over her shoulder toward Seth and shot him her best trust-me smile.

"My wife is going to walk down the aisle in Vanessa's place. Ready?" the Reverend Colby asked.

Aim . . . fire! Vanessa thought, nodding her head.

"Tum tum de da," Gloria sang as she began slowly marching up the center aisle. "Tum tum de da."

"She's humming our song," Lee said, grinning from ear to ear, winking in her direction.

Vanessa inwardly cringed at his corny joke, but managed to give him a stiff smile. Corny, but smart, she mused.

Lee had cleverly made certain they'd been in the presence of two or three people at all times. Once or twice she caught him with a quizzical expression on his face when the others weren't looking, but as the rehearsal progressed he'd relaxed and started making wisecracks.

It set Vanessa's teeth on edge to be smiling at him when she wanted nothing less than to stand up and bounce a candelabra off the top of his head. Only the certainty that Seth would finish the job for her by wrapping it around his neck like a sterling-silver bow tie kept the vacant smile on her lips.

She could almost feel Seth's dark eyes boring holes into her back. By now, the trust she'd asked for had to be stretched to the breaking point. Earlier, in The But terfly's kitchen, the pained look in his eyes had been enough to break Vanessa's heart. Charles had proudly shown her Seth's masterpiece, a gigantic wedding cake. A knot had formed in her throat that equaled the size of the iced fruitcake perched on top of the inverted champagne glasses. The cake wasn't only a labor of love, it was a monument of trust. In a husky voice she'd tried to save him the additional pain of witnessing the wedding rehearsal, but he'd politely refused to be excluded.

Vanessa folded her arms on the pew in front of her and bowed her head, resting her forehead on her arm. Just the thought of Seth's heartache made her stomach roll.

She couldn't continue to go through the motions of being Lee's bride. Not for Charlotte's sake. Not for the triumphant thrill of getting poetic justice. Not at the price Seth was having to pay.

Slowly rising to her feet, she stepped directly into Gloria's path. She took a deep breath to fortify herself, and loudly, clearly said, "Lee, I'm not going to marry you."

For long seconds there wasn't a sound, then everyone was rushing toward her, all talking at once.

"What about Charlotte?" Gloria stage-whispered.

"You can't call off the wedding!" Lee shouted.

"That's my girl!" the Colonel boomed.

Gloria had her by one elbow, Lee the other, and the Colonel and Seth were charging up the aisle. Charlotte stood in the balcony, too paralyzed by Vanessa's announcement to move.

"You heard Vanessa," Seth countered Lee. His voice was steely and dangerously low pitched. "She isn't going to marry you."

From slow motion to fast forward, Vanessa watched Lee drop her arm, cock his arm back and let his fist fly. Without time to consider the consequences, she stepped between Lee and Seth.

Nine

———

Seth swung Vanessa out of harm's way with one arm and blocked Lee's blow with the other. A red haze of fury curtained between himself and Lee's contorted face. Lee's solid blow to his arm could have seriously injured Vanessa.

"Stop it!" Charlotte screamed.

The Colonel did—with one swift punch into Lee's solar plexus. Lee crumpled to his knees, gagging. "I told you that sometimes a rip-roarin' brawl cleared the air." He hauled Lee up by the scruff of the neck, shaking him like a bag of bones. "Who's the woman running down the balcony steps?"

"I don't..." His head bobbed from side to side when the Colonel shook him again. "Charlotte. Her name's Charlotte."

"What's she doing here?"

Vanessa brushed in front of Seth. "I invited her."

"Why?" A gleam in her grandfather's eyes told Vanessa he was thoroughly enjoying himself. His eyes narrowed, then impaled Lee. "Well?"

Lee twisted himself free from the older man's grasp. Infuriated, he jerked on the hem of his jacket with one hand and straightened his tie with the other. It was apparent to all concerned that Lee was preparing to lie his way out of this predicament.

"I'm going to marry Lee tomorrow," Charlotte said from the rear of the church. She elbowed her way to Lee's side. Face-to-face, practically nose-to-nose, she asked Lee, "Right?"

Vanessa's eyes hadn't left Seth's face. She'd seen the tight rein he'd held on his temper. She'd seen his lips thin in satisfaction when she heard Lee's knees hit the carpet. Now he was smiling as Charlotte spoke. When he glanced down at her, she expected to see warmth radiating from his eyes.

His dark eyes blazed, but not with love. He was furious with her!

Had she missed something? she wondered. Turning to Lee, she answered Charlotte's question for him. "Yes, he is. He's got the marriage license. Don't be an idiot, Lee. You pride yourself on being a Southern gentleman. Don't disappoint everyone by not knowing when you've lost the war."

For half a second, Vanessa felt sorry for Lee. His pride was forcing him to nod his head. But when he looked at Charlotte standing by his side during the worst of adversities, her pity vanished.

"Will you marry me, Charlotte?" Lee muttered.

"I beg your pardon, Lee. I couldn't quite hear—"

"Marry me!"

Charlotte beamed. "Of course I'll marry you. That's why I came here. Why don't you have a little chat with the Reverend Colby while I thank everyone for helping me."

True to his heritage, Lee was beaten but unbowed. Head held high, he approached the minister and was led out of the sanctuary to the minister's office.

Throwing her arms around both Gloria's and Vanessa's necks, Charlotte bubbled, "How can I ever thank you?"

"Well, now that you've asked," Gloria replied, "I do have this absolutely gorgeous bridesmaid's dress that's going to go to waste unless I'm invited to be part of the wedding party."

"Flake," Vanessa heard the Colonel murmur.

"I'd be honored to have you in my wedding, Gloria." Willing to share her happiness with the woman who'd made it possible, she hugged Vanessa hard. "Vanessa?"

Lightly kissing Charlotte's cheek, Vanessa shook her head. "Tongues would really waggle if the bride became the bridesmaid. Tomorrow is your day." She reached backward, searching for Seth's hand, intending to announce tentative wedding plans of her own. Grabbing only air, she pivoted just in time to see him leaving the church. "Be happy," she called over her shoulder as she sprinted up the aisle.

Seth plowed down the stone church steps. He'd had to leave before he exploded. His knuckles pounded into the palm of his other hand. He ran down the street toward the Colonel's parked car, then swerved when he remembered that he'd hitched a ride to the rehearsal. He'd walk back to The Butterfly. Hell, he'd run. He needed to burn off some energy.

"Seth! Wait!" Vanessa watched him turn at the corner. In high heels she didn't stand a chance of catching up with him on foot. Frowning, she walked briskly to her car.

She couldn't imagine why she'd seen anger in his eyes. She'd called off the wedding. She'd protected Seth with her own body when Lee had taken a swing at him. Was that it? she wondered. Seth was used to fighting his own battles. Did he resent having her prevent a fight? Lee had taken the first swing. It was natural for Seth to want to throw the final punch, but, for heaven's sake—she couldn't let them duke it out in the church sanctuary!

She jerked on the handle of the car door. Locked. Intent on chasing after Seth, she'd completely forgotten that her purse was on the front pew inside the church. Frustrated by her own stupidity, she groaned aloud. She couldn't go back into the church to retrieve her purse.

"Forget something?"

She whirled around. The Colonel had taken time to light his cigar before following her. He looked a bit ridiculous marching across the street with a cigar in his mouth and a woman's purse dangling from his hand.

"Yeah," she answered, grinning. "Thanks."

"You'd better hurry. The last time I saw Seth move that fast he was leaving Charleston."

"Over my dead body," she muttered, determined to stop him. She took her purse from her grandfather's fingertips and extracted her keys. "Just for the record, Colonel. I don't have to marry him, either. But I'm going to marry him. Any objections?"

The Colonel tipped his cigar upward and smiled. "No, ma'am. I've heard reformed hellions make angelic husbands."

Vanessa laughed outright. "You ought to know, slugger."

Less than ten minutes later, Vanessa was taking the steps up to the carriage house apartment two at a time. She pounded on the screen door and called Seth's name.

"Come in," Seth shouted, not missing a motion as he packed a stack of shirts and jeans into his suitcase.

Vanessa swiftly moved through the sitting room, through the hallway, to Seth's bedroom. She halted in the doorway and leaned against the doorjamb until her heartbeat slowed. The sight of his open suitcase, half-filled, and Seth moving to and from it like an automated robot sent chills up her spine.

"Packing?"

"Yep. I've done everything that I came to do."

Vanessa bit her lower lip to keep from begging him to stay. A Monarch didn't beg! she stoutly reminded herself.

"Going back to New York?"

"For a while." Seth adeptly folded his T-shirts, underwear and socks. Busy hands were good medicine for a nasty temper.

"Let me help," she offered. Any excuse to get close to him was justifiable. She bent down and picked up the pastel-blue shirt he'd worn to the wedding rehearsal. The scent of him permeated it. She held it up by the yoke and tried to neatly fold it, but her hands were trembling, making the simple chore impossible. Her tongue bonded to the roof of her mouth.

What could she say or do to make him turn around and tell her what horrendous crime she'd committed that was causing him to leave her? Didn't he realize she'd called off the wedding because of him? Or didn't he care?

Vanessa moved beside him.

Seth crossed to the dresser.

Their eyes met in the mirror. His defiant, hers soulful.

"What are you looking at?" Seth demanded. His hands clenched into tight balls. He could feel sweat beading on the back of his neck and trickling between his shoulder blades.

"You."

The man I love, her heart communicated silently. His lips slashed into a straight line, tightly compressed. An unruly forelock had fallen across his brow. Every muscle in his neck and shoulders bulged tautly. Her eyes dropped, following each vertebra from his brawny shoulders to his narrow hips. His knees were locked, the muscles in his legs pushing against the denim fabric. He'd never looked more dangerous or more appealing.

"What do you see, Vanessa? A hunk of meat? Somebody you can tear apart with those pearly white teeth of yours without giving a thought to what he's feeling?''

His voice belied the savage accusation by barely raising above the tone of a whisper. He couldn't trust his vocal cords to vibrate louder for fear of his voice cracking with emotion.

"I see the man I love," she answered candidly.

"Love?" The feral grin he'd perfected as a teenager mocked her. His dark eyes narrowed, but they continued to lock with hers. "What a joke! You don't love me any more than you loved Lee Hayden. He was convenient, I was convenient. No difference."

Seth inwardly hated himself for lashing out at Vanessa, but he couldn't control the knot of anger that stuck in his craw like a fishhook. He was leaving, but this time he wouldn't go submissively. He'd have his say, regardless of how much it hurt both of them.

She'd been the one person in the world he'd trusted, and she'd defiled that trust.

Folding her arms across her chest, Vanessa shielded herself from his accusation. She recognized his tough, cocky stance with his lips curled for what it was—a tough shell protecting a soft heart. Intuitively she knew his accusations derived from a wound she'd unwittingly caused. Seth Kimble always struck hardest when he was hurting the most. She had to convince him that whatever wrong she'd committed, it had been done innocently.

"You're wrong, Seth. You're as wrong as my grandfather was when he convinced the judge to send you off to the service. Don't you see? You're doing the same thing to me that they did to you."

"You aren't being exiled. I'm the one leaving town," Seth refuted, hearing what she said, but refusing to listen with his heart. He wouldn't allow her to turn the situation around until he felt like sticking his tail between his legs and running off. He wouldn't allow her to act as though she were the one who had been abused.

"You're convicting me of a crime I unknowingly committed, without giving me a fair hearing, aren't you? You didn't know the other kid with you had stolen his parents' car, but you were unjustly punished. Is that what you're doing to me?"

Inch by inch, she moved toward him.

Seth's eyes could no longer meet hers, and they dropped to the dresser top. He fought the urge to rake the cosmetics off the bureau onto the floor. The sound of glass smashing to smithereens on the hardwood floor was preferable to hearing the sound of pain in her voice.

Why hadn't she stayed at the church and let him slip away without a confrontation? Hurting her was worse than maiming himself.

"Go away, Vanessa." His shoulders slumped in self-defeat. "I'm no good for you. I never have been."

She reacted to his old bitterness by grabbing his forearm and spinning him around. "Fight fair, Seth. It's okay for you to be mad as hell at me, but it's dirty fighting to hit an unarmed person—yourself."

"Please, just let me leave peacefully."

"No! You said you loved me, too. Do you think I'm going to back off? Spend the rest of my life just drifting along, wondering what I've done wrong but too damned scared to ask? Uh-uh! No, thanks! I'm going to fight tooth and nail to keep you here." Her fingernails dug into his skin, proving she meant what she said. "You're going to tell me what heinous crime I've committed."

"I trusted you." His head snapped up, and he shook her hand from his arm. "Apparently you didn't think I was worthy of your trust."

"Meaning?"

"That intricate plot to have Charlotte switch places with you. You put me through hell, lady, because you didn't trust me enough to tell me."

"I couldn't tell you."

"Because you didn't trust me."

"No, dammit! Because I didn't want you to know Lee was having an affair with another woman."

"Monarch pride!" His hands went to his hips as he shook his head. "Your pride was more important to you than trusting me. What do you think was happening to my pride while I was putting together that monstrosity of a wedding cake?"

"I was protecting you."

Seth didn't know which infuriated him the most— her not trusting him, or listening to her claim that she hadn't told him of her plans because she was protecting him.

"You almost got decked, protecting me from Lee. Take another look at me, Vanessa. Do I look like a man who needs to be bodily protected by a woman?"

Her eyes skittered over the jaw he'd thrust forward. Close up, she could see the tiny scars where men stronger than Lee had landed their punches. "No, you don't need me to physically protect you. What happened at the church was pure reflex on my part. I saw Lee start to swing and I moved between the two of you.''

Seth nodded sharply as though her answer proved what he'd been saying. They were right back where they started. She didn't trust him.

He brushed by her to finish his packing.

"I thought you'd massacre Lee if you knew he was having an affair with another woman," Vanessa blurted. "It wasn't because I didn't trust you that I didn't tell you about the plan, and it wasn't because of hurt pride. I didn't want you thrown in jail because you were protecting me!"

Seth's hands, which were holding a pair of socks, stopped in midair as if they'd suddenly turned to stone. The fact that she'd known about Lee all along finally hit him with the force of a hurricane.

While he'd been protecting her by not telling her about Lee, she'd been protecting him!

His mind jumped to what would have happened if he hadn't known about Lee and Charlotte. If the plot she'd hatched with Charlotte had succeeded—and he seriously doubted they could have carried it off—Lee and Charlotte would have wed, then left town on their honeymoon.

Leaving her free to marry a man she could trust, Seth mused, inwardly feeling as though he'd swallowed the entire fruitcake he'd baked, whole, tradition and all. No one in his entire life had loved him, trusted him enough to go to such elaborate measures to protect him from himself.

"Vanessa?" He dropped the socks, closed the suitcase and set it on the floor.

"Yes?" She'd been holding her breath, waiting for another explosion. But when he had turned around, she saw the oddest smile on his face.

He sat down on the edge of the bed, knees spread apart, and pointed to the floor. "Come here."

"Why?"

"Because I'm going to show you how much I trust you." His voice was no longer hard and cold as frozen berries. It was soft and sweet and thick as whipped cream. "C'mere."

Seated, he was far less physically intimidating than he'd been, but that didn't stop her from being wary. Carefully assessing the situation, she shuffled forward.

"Twenty-six is a bit old for corporal punishment."

"Trust me. I don't spank women." His eyes were wide open, devilry dancing in them as he looked up at her. "I protect them from bridegrooms jilted at the altar."

"I didn't jilt Lee," she protested weakly.

"That's not the rumor you'll be hearing tomorrow." Her knees were between his before his hands settled on her waist. She kneeled down between his legs until their eyes were level. "They'll be saying that that hellion Seth Kimble came back to town and stole you away from Lee."

Vanessa rested her palms on his hard thighs. "I don't think so. You and I were the only ones who didn't know he was seeing Charlotte, from what Gloria said."

"Wrong, love." He tucked a loose tendril of hair behind her ear. "You were the only one who didn't know."

"You knew?" She'd been protecting him when he'd known all along? "Why didn't you tell me?"

"Monarch pride," he answered simply.

"You'd have let me marry him rather than hurt my pride!" Her fingers curled into a ball. She used them to forcefully push his shoulders flat on the bed. "You rotten scoundrel!"

"And you say I'm the one with the temper? The one who'd land in jail for fighting?" She started to spin away from him. His hands snaked out and sprawled her indelicately on top of him. He stretched both their arms above his head. She squirmed, and he looped one leg over the backs of hers. "Tell me you're madly in love with a rotten scoundrel."

"Never."

Topsy-turvy, he rolled her over and pinned her beneath him.

"Tell me there's a certain lovable hellion that you're going to let love, honor and protect you," he demanded playfully, nipping her earlobe between his teeth.

She bucked her hips to get him off her. "You're going to need protecting when I get my hands loose, Seth Kimble. Get off me, you big galoot."

Laughing, he waggled his tongue on the ticklish spot under her ear until he heard a muffled giggle. "Tell me you'll marry me, Vanessa Monarch, and we'll protect each other...forever."

"I'll have to think about it." For maybe two or three seconds, she mused, inwardly rejoicing. His tongue was doing exquisite breathtaking things to her ear. "Aah, I'm thinking. Don't rush me."

He released her wrists and framed her face with his hands. "Rushing you now is better than kidnapping you tomorrow in front of a hundred witnesses."

"Kidnapping?" His thumb rubbing along her bottom lip was playing havoc with her breathing. The sparkle in his dark eyes had vanished. She knew he was thinking about tomorrow, what he'd have done had the wedding proceeded as planned.

"You wouldn't have made it to the church. I'd have volunteered to take you there, only I'd planned on taking a long detour via New York City."

"Did you really think I could make love with you and marry another man?"

His finger made an X over her heart. "Here, I knew you had doubts about Lee before I arrived. From what you said the first day, you and Lee were like brother and sister. After I saw him with Charlotte—"

"You saw them together?"

"Yeah. I smelled a skunk in the woodpile. Originally I'd just planned on dropping by the bank and checking Lee out. Something had to be wrong with a man who wasn't sexually interested in his future bride. His secretary told me where I'd find him."

Joan, Vanessa thought, silently identifying Lee's secretary. She'd known, too?

"When I saw Lee with Charlotte, I understood how Lee managed to keep his hands off you. I'll have to admit, I did have a helluva time keeping my hands off him. But I knew the minute Lee was seen sporting twin black eyes that I'd be right back where I started. He'd be the clean-cut, blond-headed, choirboy hero, and I'd be the criminal with the fast fists. I was in a no-win situation." He sighed, running his hand through her hair, spreading it like a halo about her face.

"You could have told me. I'd have believed you."

"I considered that option, but I knew what it would do to your pride. Gloria and I discussed telling you. Neither of us wanted to hurt you."

"You two and everybody else in Charleston," Vanessa said under her breath. "Lee's running around must have been the best kept secret in Charleston."

"Until you stood up at the church and made your announcement, I didn't know you'd seen them together." His voice held a note of recrimination.

"I was protecting you, remember? The minute I found myself wanting to kiss you like I'd never wanted to kiss Lee, I knew I had to call off the wedding. He broke our luncheon date, so I went to his place. I nearly fell down the steps on top of them when I saw Lee laying a king-size smackeroo on Charlotte."

Seth grinned at her choice of words, then immediately sobered. "It had to have hurt your pride."

"Crazy things went through my head. Everything from being outraged to wondering if there was something wrong with me." She raised upward and brushed her lips on the corner of Seth's mouth. "You eliminated my self-doubts."

"In the courtyard?"

"Mmm-hmm."

"I'd say both our self-doubts were shed that night— right along with our clothing!"

"My self-doubts, not yours. You still didn't think I had the nerve to call off the wedding. You should have known the gift of love I gave you that night can only be given to one man, once."

"A fool who's never been given a precious gift is busy looking to see if there are strings attached."

"There are strings attached," Vanessa confessed with a wide smile. Her arms lassoed around his shoulders just as she heard a car door slam below. She didn't move. Seth didn't move, either. "I told the Colonel you wouldn't be leaving Charleston unless it was over my dead body."

Seth cocked his head, listening for which direction the Colonel's footsteps moved.

"He won't come up here," Vanessa mumbled, feeling twelve instead of twenty-six. Her grandfather had caught Seth with her once before. She squirmed beneath Seth, remembering the outcome.

Shoe leather striking step treads made a liar out of her.

"You aren't going to budge, are you?" she asked when she saw a slow smile curving Seth's mouth.

"No."

"But, Seth—" Her protest was ended by a sizzling hot kiss blistering her mouth. Spicy, wild, primitive—Seth's special brand of kiss. The devil himself could have been marching up the steps and Vanessa couldn't have cared.

"You two in there!" the Colonel said as he pounded his fist on the door frame.

Seth raised his head, winked at Vanessa and called, "We're in the bedroom."

Vanessa heard the screen door squeak, then slam shut. "Have you gone stark raving crazy?"

"I'm crazy about you when your face turns the exact same shade as strawberry mousse." Seth grinned wickedly, aware of what was going through her mind. "Quit flapping your arms like a butterfly caught in a net. You don't have to protect me. Trust me. I know exactly what the Colonel is going to ask."

He'd trusted her when he believed the worst was about to happen. She had to trust him.

She heard the Colonel's footsteps marching down the hallway, smelled the odor of his infernal cigar, but her eyes never wavered from Seth's lips.

"Are you trying to seduce my granddaughter?" Seth mouthed, seconds before the Colonel opened his mouth and bellowed the question.

"Yes, sir," Seth staunchly replied. His lips smiled as they mouthed the Colonel's next question. "Do you think you're good enough to marry a Monarch?"

"Yes, sir, he is," Vanessa answered as she placed her hand on Seth's mouth. "I'd trust him with my life."

Seth kissed her fingertips and shifted to her side. The Colonel wouldn't be satisfied until he heard those words coming from him. "Yes, sir. I love her. With your permission, I want to marry her."

"Permission granted...son." Clamping his cigar between his smiling lips, he quietly closed the bedroom door.

* * * * *

MAURA SEGER

A compelling trilogy stretching from the Civil War to the twentieth century and chronicling the lives of three passionate women.

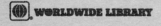

Silhouette Classics®

THE NAME SAYS IT ALL!

CLASSICS

Specially selected for you, the best books from Silhouette Intimate Moments and Silhouette Special Edition are back by popular demand. The ones you loved and the ones you missed, all written by top romance authors.

Silhouette Classics®

Don't miss the best this time around!
Look out for two Classic novels every month.

Silhouette Desire®

1989
IS THE YEAR
OF THE MAN!

What makes a romance? A special man, of course, and Silhouette Desire celebrates that fact with *twelve* of them! From Mr. January to Mr. December, every month has a tribute to the Silhouette Desire hero—our **MAN OF THE MONTH!**

Sexy, macho, charming, irritating . . . irresistible! Nothing can stop these men from sweeping you away. Created by some of your favorite authors, each man is custom-made for pleasure—*reading* pleasure—so don't miss a single one.

Mr. January is Blake Donavan in RELUCTANT FATHER by Diana Palmer
Mr. February is Hank Branson in THE GENTLEMAN INSISTS by Joan Hohl
Mr. March is Carson Tanner in NIGHT OF THE HUNTER by Jennifer Greene
Mr. April is Slater McCall in A DANGEROUS KIND OF MAN by Naomi Horton
Mr. May is Luke Harmon in VENGEANCE IS MINE by Lucy Gordon
Mr. June is Quinn McNamara in IRRESISTIBLE by Annette Broadrick

And that's only the half of it—
so get out there and find your man!

Silhouette Desire's

MAN OF THE MONTH . . .

MOM-1

Keepsake

 Harlequin Books

You're never too young to enjoy romance. Harlequin for you . . . and Keepsake, young-adult romances destined to win hearts, for your daughter.

Pick one up today and start your daughter on her journey into the wonderful world of romance.

Two new titles to choose from each month.